“Invite Me Up,” Ryder Said.

Macy arched one eyebrow, as if in control. “Why would I do that?”

His voice, when he found it, was rough. “There’s something I want to talk to you about.”

“I don’t think talking’s what you have in mind.”

“Sure, just because I want to talk doesn’t mean I’m not aching to touch you.” *To kiss you. To taste you.*

Macy’s pupils dilated as Ryder leaned over and brushed his lips across hers.

Her mouth yielded, opened to him. Drunk on her exotic scent, he lifted his hands to cup her face, finding her cheeks were like silk under his palms. He felt her hands on his shoulders, lightly, then more assured as they traveled an exquisite path to his neck before her fingers tangled in his hair. He was lost—

A flash went off, lighting up the lobby, and Ryder pulled back, blinking.

The paparazzi had found him.

Dear Reader,

Chocolate is one of my very favorite things (some might even say I have a little addiction). And I'm a firm believer in its romantic properties, be it dark or milk chocolate; crisp from the fridge or melting on the tongue; plain or enrobing butterscotch pieces.

So, as you can imagine, the idea of combining chocolate with a passionate romance was irresistible.

All I needed was the perfect hero for my chocolate story. Enter Ryder Bramson. He quickly became one of my favorite heroes with his quiet intensity, the strength of his integrity and his utter respect for Macy. I developed quite the crush on Ryder, but unfortunately he had eyes only for his heroine.

I hope you enjoy Ryder and Macy's story. I recommend you read it with chocolate close to hand!

Rachel

RACHEL BAILEY

AT THE BILLIONAIRE'S BECK AND CALL?

Published by Silhouette Books
America's Publisher of Contemporary Romance

If you purchased this book without a cover you should be aware that this book is stolen property. It was reported as "unsold and destroyed" to the publisher, and neither the author nor the publisher has received any payment for this "stripped book."

Recycling programs for this product may not exist in your area.

ISBN-13: 978-0-373-73052-0

AT THE BILLIONAIRE'S BECK AND CALL?

Copyright © 2010 by Rachel Robinson

All rights reserved. Except for use in any review, the reproduction or utilization of this work in whole or in part in any form by any electronic, mechanical or other means, now known or hereafter invented, including xerography, photocopying and recording, or in any information storage or retrieval system, is forbidden without the written permission of the editorial office, Silhouette Books, 233 Broadway, New York, NY 10279 U.S.A.

This is a work of fiction. Names, characters, places and incidents are either the product of the author's imagination or are used fictitiously, and any resemblance to actual persons, living or dead, business establishments, events or locales is entirely coincidental.

This edition published by arrangement with Harlequin Books S.A.

For questions and comments about the quality of this book please contact us at Customer_eCare@Harlequin.ca.

® and TM are trademarks of Harlequin Books S.A., used under license. Trademarks indicated with ® are registered in the United States Patent and Trademark Office, the Canadian Trade Marks Office and in other countries.

Visit Silhouette Books at www.eHarlequin.com

Printed in U.S.A.

Books by Rachel Bailey

Silhouette Desire

Claiming His Bought Bride #1992
The Blackmailed Bride's Secret Child #1998
At the Billionaire's Beck and Call? #2039

RACHEL BAILEY

developed a serious book addiction at a young age (via Peter Rabbit and Jemima Puddleduck) and has never recovered. Just how she likes it. She went on to gain degrees in psychology and social work, but is now living her dream—writing romance for a living.

She lives on a piece of paradise on Australia's Sunshine Coast with her hero and four dogs, and loves to sit with a dog or two, overlooking the trees and reading books from her ever-growing to-be-read pile.

Rachel would love to hear from you and can be contacted through her Web site, www.rachelbailey.com.

This book is dedicated to Emily May, who flew in like an angel when we were in such need of her. And to Sandii, Barb, Alison L, Alison A, Annie and Mum, who all provided practical help as well as their support. And the staff of the Royal Brisbane and Women's Hospital's Cancer Care Services. And to everyone who sent us thoughts, cards, hugs, prayers and wishes. You all helped immeasurably.

Huge thanks to Charles Griemsman for your insight and skill. You're a pleasure to work with and your chocolate appreciation says much about your character.

And, as always, thank you to the fabulous Jenn Schober.

One

He was staring at her again.

Her boss, Ryder Bramson.

Macy broke away from his unsettling gaze and re-focused on the meeting at hand. And yet her eyes drifted back to the Armani-clad man with the deep frown-line between his eyebrows. She knew Ryder Bramson by name—who didn't?—but she'd seen him in the flesh for the first time today when he and his team had arrived in Melbourne from the States to check on the progress of this special project.

At six foot three, with closely cropped brown hair and rugged features, she had a feeling he'd stand out wherever he was, yet that hardly explained the unexpected thrum of desire that had resonated through her bloodstream at her first glimpse of the man she'd been working under for the past two weeks. Or the way her breath caught slightly every time his coffee-brown eyes flicked to hers during the introductions.

Sitting tall and broad in his chair, he watched her now, his head turned at an arrogant forty-five-degree angle to the left as if no one was worthy of him looking them squarely in the face. Unbelievably disconcerting.

It wasn't as if she'd never been stared at before—it'd been one of the few constants in her life. Before she'd escaped to Australia at eighteen, she'd lived in a golden cage of wealth, luxury and limelight. The eldest of two children of a corporate giant and a Hollywood actress, she'd always drawn more than her fair share of unwelcome interest.

But this man's stare was different. More intense. More focused. As if he could see through every defensive layer of protection she'd ever constructed.

Macy shivered and looked back at the statistics in front of her.

Her accountant finished his address and, despite her straying thoughts, Macy smoothly took her cue. "You'll see the figures we've collected on each of Chocolate Diva's potential competitors in this report."

She passed a pile of bound documents to her personal assistant, who stood and distributed them to the people at the table.

Ryder accepted his and, without a glance, passed it directly to his secretary. "Tell me in your own words," he said, his voice deep and authoritative.

Not missing a beat, Macy explained her findings so far. "If we're to expand into the Australian marketplace we'll need to find a niche in the already well-supplied market of chocolate products. Taking our research and forecasts into consideration, we will likely recommend beginning with three of our current products, some adapted for the

Australian consumer, inserted into current retail outlets. Also two brand-name shops, one each in the Sydney and Melbourne city centers."

She'd spent two weeks living and breathing this project before today's meeting with Ryder Bramson and his entourage. She knew the figures by heart. She and her small staff of two had put in ridiculously long days, cramming more into two weeks than even she had thought possible.

Yet, Ryder didn't seem impressed. His strongly featured face remained impassive, unmoved...except for every so often when he pierced her with that penetrating stare.

Like now.

Her skin tightened across her entire body and her pulse kicked up a notch. But she schooled her expression to be as unresponsive as his, and continued with her explanations of the projected profit and loss analysis. She'd bet good money that stare was one of the reasons for his phenomenal success with his family's food empire—adversaries would always be off balance and employees desperate to perform their best for him.

She, however, would conceal how his calculating appraisal affected her. She'd grown up surrounded by powerful, emotionally remote men, starting with her father. The man who'd distanced himself from her when she was only thirteen and her mother had just died. Her understanding that in his grief-stricken state he couldn't cope with her resemblance to her mother hadn't lessened the pain. Especially when he'd been kinder to her sister, whose looks and personality didn't remind him so much of his dead wife.

Macy squared her shoulders. That experience had changed her, made her what she was. A strong, independent woman.

She could handle Mr. Bramson and his stare.

Glancing down at her laptop, she clicked a button and brought up a graph to show her point more clearly. It appeared on the LCD screens built into the conference table in front of the seven other people at the meeting. Six of them lowered their gazes to read.

The seventh kept his focus squarely on her, his head turned to the side at that almost insolent angle.

Macy felt a flush of nerves creep through her system—something she rarely felt in a business meeting, a place where she prided herself on being prepared and in control. Yet at this meeting, her boss barely seemed interested in the results he'd hired her to find. And when he looked at her like that, she found herself thinking more like a flesh and blood woman than a businesswoman. Her skin heated, her breathing became shallow.

No. She would not be sidetracked by biological responses to a man. Especially not now. There was no way she'd miss the chance to be Chocolate Diva's first Australian CEO.

She met his gaze. "Is there a problem with your screen, Mr. Bramson?"

He lifted his right eyebrow—the first reaction he'd revealed since arriving in the building thirty-five minutes earlier. "I haven't crossed the Pacific to look at graphs and reports that I could have studied from the comfort of my own office, Ms. Ashley."

Macy nodded, ignoring the unease in her stomach. Of course he hadn't. She flicked a switch and the screens went blank. Time for a change of direction—she was nothing if not flexible. Adaptable. Promotable.

When he'd headhunted her from her previous position—working for the corporate raider Damon Blakely, overseeing acquisitions of small companies—Ryder had made her a promise. During their phone interview, he'd said if this two-month project went well, she'd be in the running for the top job at Chocolate Diva—the high-end chocolate and candy brand—as it opened its doors in Australia. A job she wanted badly. The sort of job she'd been working toward since she graduated top of her class in her business degree. A major step toward her career goal of running a company at least the size of her father's.

So if the boss didn't want to be bothered reading reports, she was more than fine with that option. "We've prepared some samples of possible product variations for your team to try."

He'd been examining the other staff members at the table, and now turned his head in a slow, deliberate move to look at her again, his intense physical presence seeming to reach out and touch her from across the table.

She held his gaze, unwilling to blink or show the smallest sign of intimidation. "Perhaps you and your staff would like to take the afternoon to recover from jetlag, and we'll resume first thing in the morning with the product tastings."

His right brow again arched, as if Ryder Bramson never needed time to recover from any experience. He probably didn't.

Macy waited. It was his move.

Finally Ryder dipped his chin in one slow, yet precise nod. "If the product samples are ready, I'll try them now. The U.S. team can go back to the hotel and be back by 9:00 a.m. sharp."

The men and women in suits began assembling their papers and lifting briefcases, but Ryder's clear, deep voice carried across their noise. "Ms. Ashley, I have a phone call to make. I'll meet you back in here in ten minutes."

Macy nodded then resumed gathering the reports and folders off the table in front of her and stood.

Shaun, a lean, gray-haired American from Missouri, whispered on the way out the door, "Don't let him put you off, it's just his way. He's a good boss, but at home, they call him The Machine."

Macy nodded discreetly as Shaun peeled off in another direction. That was perfectly okay with her. She liked to focus on her work, do the best job she could. Faux friendships that often arose in workplaces were nothing more than a distraction, and she'd never been the gossip-at-the-water-cooler type.

In fact, it seemed Ryder Bramson might be the ideal boss...as long as she could contain her reactions to his gaze. Even now she could feel the pulse at her throat, the remnants of a warm shiver trailing down her spine.

Definitely a bad thing.

But she'd pandered to enough imaginings about her boss in the short time since they met. It was time to stop.

Ten minutes later, Macy looked around the meeting room, making sure everything was in place. She and her assistant, Tina, had collected ingredients yesterday to give Ryder's team a general idea of how the products could be adapted.

Tina walked in with a bowl of fruit pieces and laid it on the table. "How do you want to run this?"

Macy had planned the exercise for a group but it shouldn't be a problem to downscale. She moved a bowl of dried lychees an inch to the left to make everything line up more squarely. "While you make up the samples and hand them to Mr. Bramson, I'll explain the choices."

"Sounds good," Tina said as she turned on the chocolate fountain they'd filled with their own brand's imported rich, dark chocolate.

Movement in the corner of her eye caught her attention, and Macy turned. She took in Ryder Bramson filling the doorway—he'd removed both the charcoal business jacket and tie, and rolled up the sleeves of his teal-blue shirt. The dark hair on his strong forearms covered tanned skin, leading down to large, square hands with long fingers. Unbidden, the image of those hands roaming her skin filled her mind, those arms wrapped around her, pulling her close. Her gaze traveled up to his face, his full bottom lip, then to his eyes, which were regarding her with a lazy appraisal of their own.

Macy swallowed. Stepped back. Put a chair between them.

Tina looked up and smiled—the picture of a professional reaction. "Ah, Mr. Bramson, we're ready for you."

His eyes lingered on Macy for another long moment before they flicked to her assistant. "Tina, isn't it? Looks like you've done a great job here, but I won't keep you from your work. I'm sure Ms. Ashley will be able to help me."

Macy's heartbeat stuttered. She glanced at Tina and saw the question in her eyes. She knew Tina was rushing to get the information on potential retail sites together, and, as Ryder was the only person coming for the tasting now, it made sense for Macy to do this alone. But with the sexual charge in the room, with the way her insides melted every time her boss looked at her, she could well do with a chaperone—

Macy stopped herself mid-thought. What was she thinking? She'd never let herself be diverted from her goals before, and she wasn't about to start now. She closed her eyes, took a breath, then opened them and smiled at Tina. "It's okay, I'll be fine here."

Tina paused a moment as if to reassure herself she really could leave, then bustled from the room.

Ryder strolled over and surveyed the food on the table before again meeting her eyes. "Where do you want me?"

She stilled, but Ryder's strong face remained impassive, dark eyes focused on her, no sign of teasing or flirting visible. Brilliant, now she was reading double entendres into his words.

She found a polite smile and pointed to the head of the table. "There will be fine."

Ryder took his seat and she sat in the chair to his right, in easy reach of all the ingredients, then slipped into the speech she'd been preparing in her mind. "The Diva Truffle Bar has tested well and is unique. At this stage we believe it will be able to enter the Australian market in its current form." The bar—crushed almond and honeycomb in a chocolate truffle, coated in their own brand chocolate—would be as much a hit here as overseas if her research was correct. "We've run some preliminary focus groups and the feedback from the tastings was overwhelmingly positive."

Ryder steepled his fingers under his chin, elbows on the armrests of his chair. But said nothing.

The silence threatened to stretch and leave her in the unfamiliar position of being flustered, so she took a breath and forged on with her spiel.

"The second product we're investigating as an option is Diva Drops." The dried fruit pieces smothered in a thick layer of their dark chocolate was their second highest selling line in the U.S., after the Truffle Bar. "Given your preference for Australian production using Australian products where possible, we might need to adapt some varieties. The cherries, cranberries and blueberries are harder to source here so we're looking into the viability of some locally grown fruit."

Ryder tipped his chin to the bowls in front of them. "Such as mango."

Macy nodded and picked up a piece of dried mango on a toothpick then held it beneath the stream of the chocolate fountain. "This is dried Bowen mango. It's in plentiful supply in the north during the summer and we have some early feelers out now with growers."

She waited till the chocolate solidified, then handed the toothpick to him, realizing too late that there was very little room on the end of the pick for both sets of fingers. His thumb and forefinger encircled hers, capturing her hand with a gentle clasp. Time seemed to still as her body reacted to the touch, from the heat in her hand right down to a tug of desire deep in the core of her being.

She'd been thinking of his hands only minutes before and his fingers were so firm, his palm radiating such warmth on the back of her hand that she was glad she was already sitting down.

Then he moved to grasp the toothpick at the very end and she let go. He lifted it slowly and as the chocolate and mango reached higher, his tongue appeared and took the food into the dark depths of his mouth before he slid the pick out through closed lips.

With a start, Macy realized she'd been staring, so she began stabbing toothpicks in other pieces of fruit, but this time, arranged them on a plate instead of handing them to him.

Keeping her eyes glued to her task, she asked, "What did you think?"

There was no response as she put several more pieces of dried mango through the chocolate fountain then onto his plate. Her eyes drifted back to him. He was watching her.

He cleared his throat. "Delicious."

The sensuality in his voice was unmistakable but Macy had no choice but to ignore it, despite the protestations of her body. She couldn't afford to ruin this opportunity. That Australian CEO position had her name on it, and if she got the job, hopefully Ryder Bramson would remain her boss for a long time. She needed to keep this professional relationship working optimally.

She pushed the plate in front of him. "Other fruits in plentiful supply are pineapple, lychees and strawberries. Additionally—" she picked up the silver sugar tongs and pulled another bowl over "—we're considering adding mint leaves to the range." She ran the fresh mint leaf under the stream of chocolate, but before she could place it on his plate, Ryder laid his palm out for the delicacy.

She looked up, sure her boss was the type who'd want to minimize mess, but he nodded so she laid the leaf into the palm of his hand. Making sure not to watch him consume this one—staying professional—she grabbed a couple of napkins and put them beside his plate.

He wiped the chocolate remnants from his hand, then sampled an assortment of the other morsels from his plate. She could feel him watching her as he tasted and chewed, but she found things for her hands to do. Her pulse fluttered but thankfully her hands were steady.

"Very good," his deep voice rumbled. "You said you'd be recommending three lines. The Truffle Bar, these variations of the Drops and…?"

"And the basic sampler tray. The current five fillings in

the sampler should be suitable, but we'll run more focus groups before finalizing that recommendation."

A knock sounded at the open door and Tina walked in. "How's it going in here? Do you need me?"

Ryder leaned back in his chair, eminently comfortable in his new domain. "No, Ms. Ashley has taken good care of me."

Her skin heated as if the timbre of his voice, the intensity of his gaze could reach across and touch her. Caress her. Stroke her. She suspected that if he beckoned her now with the crook of a finger, she'd go without a second thought.

Thank goodness they'd be working on opposite sides of the globe most of the time. He was unexpectedly dangerous to her composure.

She flicked her hair over her shoulder, glancing around the table, at the ingredients they'd been through. "Actually, unless you want to keep tasting, I've pretty much shown you everything."

Ryder nodded once and stood. "These options are good. Tina, tomorrow you can run them past Shaun and the team." He turned back to Macy. "Ms. Ashley, I'd like to see you for a moment alone. In my office, please."

A shiver of excitement skittered along her spine despite knowing his request was professional—of course he'd want to talk to the team leader.

She stood taller and nodded. "Certainly."

This was her opportunity to impress him—an opportunity she'd been looking forward to. But that was before she'd met him and felt how he could effortlessly bring her body zinging to life.

Would the effect be magnified once they were closeted in an office, alone?

* * *

Ryder stood behind the polished wooden desk in his temporary office and stared down at the cruising boats negotiating the ribbon of the Yarra River.

Macy was perfect. The woman he'd crossed the globe to meet had the face of an angel, the body of a Venus and a spine of steel. He'd have married her just to buy her father's company, but all evidence now pointed to him enjoying this marriage.

Marriage.

Macy would be his wife.

Ryder sucked in a satisfied breath.

He knew he was cut from the same cloth as his own father—he'd lost count of the number of times people had told him that—knew he was incapable of love, especially the forever kind. So a practical marriage would suit him perfectly—he'd have companionship and raise a family, sidestepping the love issue.

He heard Macy's voice, sweet as birdsong, coming down the corridor, talking rapidly to one of her staff, and he shook aside his wandering thoughts. One step at a time, no point getting ahead of himself.

Then she stood in the doorway, looking impossibly beautiful, awaiting his instruction. Her mysterious hazel eyes assessed him and her curtain of dark brown hair draped her shoulders like satin. Long, toned legs showed below the skirt of her suit, but he tried not to look.

He indicated with a hand that she could enter and she moved to stand in front of him, seemingly so delicate. For one crazy moment, he lost himself in the desire to explore her delicateness more intimately. To step forward—

"You wanted to see me, Mr. Bramson?"

Her words brought his attention back to the meeting…

and his eyes back from her legs. He swallowed hard. "Call me Ryder."

Her only reaction was to flick her hair behind a shoulder encased in a pearl-gray business jacket. "Ryder."

"You've done well with this project. I don't have to tell you that the expansion of this arm of our company into Australia depends on your conclusions, but I see it's in good hands from the work you've completed."

"Thank you." She didn't look pleased by the praise, though she didn't look displeased, either. Her expression was too aloof for either, almost feline in the way her nose tipped up, the way her eyes blinked slowly. He liked it.

He sank his hands deep into his trouser pockets. "Have you had any problems?"

She raised a slim shoulder dismissively. "Nothing I couldn't deal with."

Ryder allowed a ghost of a smile. Perfect answer. He had to admit, he already liked her more than any woman he'd dated. Since he'd decided to marry her three weeks ago—immediately after the reading of his father's will—he'd done a thorough background check and found that she seemed a good match for him. They both had high-profile, complicated families, and they both steered away from those families and the publicity surrounding them as much as possible.

But the bottom line was, this marriage needed to go ahead so he could buy her father's company, including its stock in his own family's company. If they had a connection, a spark, that was icing. Since—as he'd discovered at the recent reading of his father's will—his father had split his majority share of stock in Bramson Holdings between his legitimate and illegitimate families, the stakes were high. His father had begun in food, then diversified into hotels when he'd realized he would need unrelated career paths for his sons. Ryder had always expected that his half brothers would inherit Bramson Hotels, and he would inherit Bramson Food Holdings, which he's spent his entire working life strengthening.

Or that, as the legitimate son, he would get it all.

But what had happened after his father's unexpected death was a mess. Neither he nor his half brothers owned enough stock in the parent company to hold outright control by themselves, turning the boardroom into a battle ground. Damn shortsighted of his father, but the upshot was, Ryder needed to fix this, fast.

His mother had stoically suffered the scandals and his father's emotional neglect through her marriage and in return she'd been publicly humiliated after her husband's death. One thing Ryder could guarantee—he would acquire enough stock to claim a majority in his own right and gain control of the board. Set everything to right again.

Macy's father's company was a key in that plan. Ian Ashley's company owned a chunk of stock in Bramson Holdings. A chunk that Ryder himself would own, as soon as he could buy Ashley International. And then he'd be within sight of that clear majority of stock.

Time to place his proposition on the table. And to do that, he needed to see her one-on-one.

He knew her father hadn't told her about the secret condition of sale, that he wanted the new owner to marry one of his daughters. Seemed he was an old-school businessman and wanted to pass the company to a male heir. Since he only had daughters, he wanted to sell to a son-in-law who would, in turn, produce a grandson to inherit. Initially Ryder had resisted the marriage demand that accompanied the contract of sale on principle, but his father's will had changed everything. Now owning the stock that Ashley International held was nonnegotiable.

So, given that Macy was in the dark about her father's plans, Ryder had decided it'd be best to ease into things—to ensure his offer didn't come completely out of the blue. Of course it would still seem sudden to her—he couldn't help that. But if he was right about her, she was practical enough to appreciate the offer on its merits—he'd be a faithful husband, he was financially stable even without the inheritance, and he'd be a good father. And, to ensure her assent, he was prepared to offer her whatever she wanted, be that a house on the French Riviera, a company of her own, or whatever else she desired.

He strode across the office to shut the door, then returned to the desk, leaning a hip on the edge. Macy didn't bat an eyelash at the closed door, showing again that she was perfect for his lifestyle—unflappable.

"Macy, I'd like to see you somewhere away from the office." She opened her mouth, but he spoke first. "Have a drink with me tonight."

The pulse at the base of her throat fluttered and she didn't quite meet his eyes. "I'm not sure tonight is good."

Undeterred, he inclined his head toward the window's city view. "Where's the best place to have a drink in this city?"

She blinked. "Probably The Jazz Room. But I have no interest in mixing business with my personal life, Mr. Bramson."

"Ryder."

She drew herself up even straighter. "Ryder. If you'd like to discuss work matters, I'd be happy to—"

"I don't want to discuss work matters," he interrupted. "I'm asking you out on a date."

Her lips compressed into a flat line. "I'd prefer you didn't do that."

He'd expected resistance, and it didn't worry him. In fact, he'd rather confront any issues between them early.

He angled his head to the reports stacked on his desk. "Because I'm your boss?"

She held his gaze, unflinching. "Among other reasons."

"Well, let's deal with that one first. I'm not asking you out as your boss. I'm asking as a man who's seen a beautiful woman and wants to have a drink with her, even though it's slightly inappropriate." Make that incredibly inappropriate in the modern workplace for him to ask out an employee. But this was hardly an everyday situation. "I want you to know I've never done this before, but I'm compelled to make an exception here."

Her hazel eyes focused on his mouth for a fleeting moment, and every nerve ending in his lips leaped to life.

"It's impossible for me to forget you're my boss. You're holding a potential promotion in your hands and I'd rather not complicate that issue."

He smiled. Integrity. Such an attractive quality. "What if I gave you that promotion now? If I said you'll definitely be the CEO of Chocolate Diva's Australian operation?"

Her eyes flared and her lips parted before she brought herself back under control. "Then I'd say we've already complicated things. I want that promotion but I don't want a single question in anyone's mind about how I got it."

He pushed off the desk, bringing him to stand in front

of her…within touching distance. "We don't have to tell anyone."

She flicked her long hair over her shoulder. "That's hardly the point. I'll know."

He hadn't expected she'd accept the unearned promotion—if she'd wanted the easy route she'd still be at home with daddy's money like her sister. But he was still relieved she'd turned him down. He'd prefer his wife to have principles, even if it did make this stage of the negotiations more challenging.

He reached for her hand and held it lightly between his. No pressure, just holding. And yet her skin touching his set off a sizzling heat that traveled through his veins all the way to his toes. For one extraordinary moment, he forgot the pressure to marry, forgot the company buyout, forgot the inheritance, and just wanted.

Wanted *her.*

As he watched, a blush stole up her décolletage, along her throat and bloomed on her cheeks. *She felt it, too.* The pull to kiss her delectable lips, to taste her, was almost overwhelming. His skin tightened and his lungs labored, but he couldn't get carried away. Couldn't count his chickens before they hatched.

He needed to marry her, not entice her into his bed.

Hauling himself back, he cleared his throat. "What if I promise our date won't affect your promotion, that no one else will know, and that it will just be one drink?"

Her skin was so soft he couldn't help but run a thumb across the back of the hand he still held, then over her palm. He watched as her pupils dilated. She was wavering.

"One drink, Macy. No torture involved." He gave her a half smile. Damn, she was beautiful.

Then she withdrew her hand and nodded, back to being

cool and businesslike. "I'll meet you at the bar. Seven o'clock."

"Looking forward to it," he said before she turned and strode from his office. "More than you know," he murmured to the empty room.

He tapped a thumb to his bottom lip, still prickling with awareness of her. If he could get her to agree to his plan, if he could convince her, then it'd be full steam ahead.

And he had a gut feeling that it would be. That he'd just made a date with his future wife.

Two

At seven o'clock, Macy stood outside The Jazz Room, taking in the scene—an upmarket cocktail bar with live jazz, and a deep room full of beautiful people in their glamorous best. Muted red walls surrounded the almost-capacity crowd who sat on tall stools at the gleaming bar or at polished silver tables.

She spotted Ryder sitting at the bar, and was uncharacteristically nervous for the second time in one day. She was on a date with Ryder Bramson. She'd always been so careful about keeping her work and private life separate, yet she'd agreed to meet *her boss* socially.

It wasn't the first time she'd been hit on by a colleague or employer, but it never got any easier to rebuff. Ryder had quickly moved past her first line of defense—her aloof exterior—and now she had to play very carefully.

Rejecting the boss was just as bad a career move as sleeping with him.

In effect, she was cornered.

Ryder saw her and unfurled his long frame from the stool and strode toward her, purposeful intent oozing from his whole body. Her knees felt weak and she locked them to keep from swaying.

He stopped near enough for her to smell his clean woodsy scent, to feel the heat from his body, to see the shiny-smooth skin of his jaw where he'd recently shaved.

Ryder bent to kiss her cheek and she was surprised he'd do something so familiar. Surprised at the tingling on the side of her face where his lips had touched.

"You look beautiful," he murmured.

His voice was a note deeper than it'd been in his office, and she felt it reverberate through her body. And there was something reassuring about his American accent. She was used to being the only American in the room, surrounded by Australian accents. Her eyes were drawn to his mouth, wanting him to say something else just to hear him speak again.

Oh, who was she kidding? This was *nothing* like when she'd been hit on before. Which only meant she had to tread with even more caution—the danger of forgetting her self-imposed boundaries was greater.

She'd been burned far too many times by people ready to sell her out, or walk away when times got tough, to trust again. Everyone had an angle, or they were only looking out for themselves. Even her own father, the person she should be able to depend on utterly, had distanced himself from her when she'd needed him the most—as a thirteen-year-old girl who'd just lost her mother.

So she'd accept Ryder's compliment but not read anything much into it.

She ran her tongue over dry lips. "Thank you."

She saw him watch the action, then move his gaze slowly up to her eyes. "Do you want to sit at the bar or take a table?"

Glad for a reason to break eye contact, she scanned the room. "The tables down the back are quieter."

He put a hand on her waist and guided her toward the back of the room. As they wove their way through the tables, Johnny, a waiter who'd served her here before, was delivering drinks to a group of customers. He saw her and winked before continuing to place the brightly colored cocktails on the table.

As she spared him a brief smile, Macy thought she'd caught a faint scowl marring Ryder's features but when she looked fully at him, there was no sign.

Ryder found a table in a corner that had a modicum of privacy. He pulled her chair out for her to sit, then turned to take his own seat, giving her a brief view of his back, so broad in the moss-green shirt, and exquisitely tapered down to his black trousers. For a man who had sat virtually motionless through the meeting today, he moved with masculine grace.

"You come here regularly?" Ryder's voice held the first hint of curiosity she'd heard from him. Strange that he hadn't seemed as curious about her reports—detailing launch expenses in the millions—as her social life.

Macy shrugged one shoulder as she scanned the drinks menu. "Occasionally."

The live jazz was always exceptional, and sometimes when she'd finished a long day at work, after eating takeaway at her desk, all she wanted was to be lost in a dimly lit crowd for one drink. To unwind before going home.

Ryder didn't respond for one minute, then two. But she wouldn't look up from the list of drinks. She could feel him watching her—the air was charged with the tension of it—another tactic that probably worked well for him with employees. She continued to casually read the cocktail options.

Finally, he spoke. "Why do I get the feeling you don't talk much about yourself?"

She smiled, closed the drinks list and laid it on the silver tabletop. "I'll have a margarita."

Without looking around, he held up a finger. Johnny appeared and Ryder ordered her margarita plus a martini, no olive.

Once Johnny left, Ryder cleared his throat. "What made you settle in Melbourne?"

"I like it here."

"You obviously didn't move for the weather. Hot as hell today, yet arctic winds on the way over here tonight." He smiled ruefully.

She recrossed her legs under the table, irritated that he'd been here less than a day and was already finding fault with her adopted home. But annoyance was another reaction she couldn't show her boss. "Actually, I like the weather. Makes me feel like I'm not stuck in one place all the time. The trick is to dress in layers."

"Useful local information."

Johnny returned back with their drinks, and she gave him a quick smile. Waiter and customer—a nice, uncomplicated relationship, just how she liked them.

Then she looked across at her date—a more complicated, tangled relationship she couldn't imagine. But she smiled at him, too, and accepted her glass. "Thank you."

"Believe me, it's my pleasure." He tasted his martini and winced. "Too dry."

Macy slowly twirled her glass, looking for the perfect

place on the salt-encrusted rim to sample her drink. A much better option than looking at the man across from her. If he'd been anyone other than her boss, this might have been playing out differently…but he was.

He swallowed a mouthful of his drink then sat back in his seat. "Tell me something about yourself."

Macy sipped her margarita then licked the salt from her lips. This was the exact problem with being out socially with a colleague—the sharing of personal information. The press had shared her personal information with the world most of her life. It'd left a bitter taste in her mouth.

She tapped a fingertip on the stem of her glass. "Ryder, don't pretend you don't know who I am."

Even if her face hardly ever ran in the media nowadays, her name wouldn't slip past a man as savvy and intelligent as Ryder. Her father worked in a similar industry and her sister was in the glossy magazines most weeks. Her surname was hardly low profile.

His eyes held hers with intensity. "I know what family you come from. I know a little bit about your childhood, like most Americans. But you're wrong. I don't know who *you* are." Ryder stretched his legs to the side of the table. "But I'd like to."

Macy expelled a long breath. This farce had gone on long enough. She'd thought she could play this game—one date with the boss, but she'd been wrong. Every moment this went on, she was getting in deeper into her own personal catch-22: she couldn't get involved with him and she couldn't rebuff his efforts to get involved. Either way she'd possibly offend him and kiss her promotion goodbye. She had to say something now before she was completely out of her depth.

She flicked her hair over a shoulder and met his gaze.

"Ryder, I know I said I'd meet you here tonight, but I have to tell you, I'm uncomfortable about this."

He straightened in his chair, frowning. "Have I done something to make you uncomfortable?"

Her stomach dipped. Now she *had* offended him. The man who would decide her promotion.

She held a palm out. "No, that's the thing—you don't have to do anything. You're my boss. You pay my wage and hold a potential promotion in your hands, so I can't relax."

Ryder leaned closer. "I understand your concern. I've never done this kind of thing before, either." His voice dipped. "Here and now, I'm not your boss. I'm just a man."

Macy hesitated. She needed no reminder he was a man. Every feminine instinct she had screamed the fact. But he was her employer, too. "That's not possible. You're my boss whether you want to think about it right now or not. It's inescapable."

He raised one brow. "What if we don't try to escape it? What if we try to build on it?" His eyes darkened in a depth of emotion that took her breath away. It transformed his features from rugged to something beautiful. She wanted to reach out and touch his lips, run her hands along his strong jaw. She'd never reacted with this intensity to a man before.

Her body screamed *yes*, but she didn't, couldn't, say the word.

Instead she gave herself an internal shake. Maybe it was time to go home. "I don't think this is working."

Ryder inclined his head. "I agree. My understanding of a date includes some small talk about ourselves. If you don't want to talk about yourself, how about I talk a bit about me?"

Macy hesitated on the edge of her seat, half wanting to leave, half wanting to hear what he'd say. Like her, he was famous for not giving media interviews, and from the comment that one of his staff had made today about him being The Machine, she suspected it wasn't only the media he refused to be open with.

Apparently taking her silence as consent, Ryder took a sip of his martini, swallowed, then began. "I suspect you know I was born in Rhode Island and that I grew up there and in New York City."

She nodded, settling back into her seat now he'd made the decision for her about staying. She'd also heard about the open secret of his half brothers—would he go as far as mentioning them? From what she knew of him, it wasn't likely.

"Although my parents were married, my father was absent, so I was raised by my mother." A flash of a frown creased his forehead—too quick for her to be completely sure she'd seen it. But something told her that there was carefully guarded pain inside that statement. And the girl inside her who'd lost her mother understood.

She relaxed her face and body into an empathetic smile. "Your mother did a good job."

One corner of his mouth turned up in acknowledgment of the compliment before he took another mouthful of his drink. "My father had a second family—a mistress and two sons. I'd seen them around on occasion, but I met them for the first time at my father's funeral and then again at the will reading."

She paused, not quite believing what he'd just shared. "I saw something about that in the papers. I'm sorry."

"Thank you." He met her gaze for a moment before finishing his drink and pushing the glass to the side of the table. "His death was unexpected but our relationship wasn't particularly friendly."

"That doesn't mean it's not a shock." Her mind flew back to when she'd heard the worst news of her life and she felt the sting of emotion in her eyes that always accompanied the memory. She paused until she had it under control before continuing. "My mother died in a plane crash when I was thirteen."

"I can't imagine how you got through that," he said, voice rough. "You must have been devastated."

She'd wanted to curl up and *die.* Even now, just thinking about it, her insides were like a black hole that sucked in and destroyed any sign of joy.

She closed her eyes for a long moment, willing herself back from that place of despair before opening them again and nodding. "More than devastated. My father and sister turned to each other, and I—" *learned to never rely on anyone* "—learned to cope with life on my own."

She shook her head, banishing the thoughts, and changed the subject. "Do you wish you'd had siblings to grow up with?"

He opened his mouth, about to reply, then frowned and shut it again. She had the feeling he'd been about to offer her a standard reply, but for some reason had changed his mind.

When he spoke, his voice was pitched even lower than usual. "I used to, when I was a boy. But I don't think I would have made a good brother."

Her heart softened, honored that she'd been given this gift of truth from a man seemingly unused to bestowing it. "I think anyone would be lucky to have you."

Ryder's dark eyes changed, sparked, and the awareness that had been simmering between them leaped to life.

Her insides melted.

She watched Ryder swallow then reach across the table and lay his hand on hers.

Her blood pounded through her veins and she felt the world slow to a stop. Noises retreated until the only sound she was aware of was her own breath. There was no one but the two of them, connected through their hands on a polished metal table.

Eyes locked on his, she turned her wrist so their hands lay palm to palm. The burning heat from his hand suffused hers and traveled throughout her body, bringing goose bumps across her skin and desire coiling low in her belly.

His chest rose and fell in the same erratic rhythm as hers. His lips were slightly parted, ready to speak…or kiss. And with startling clarity she realized she wanted his kiss more than she'd ever wanted anything. Wanted to hear him whisper sweet words in her ear, to lose herself in his embrace.

Then he whispered, "Macy," and the world came crashing back with reality.

Spell broken, she lowered her eyes and extricated her hand from his gentle clasp, leaving it to lie in her lap. Ryder slid his hand across the table to grasp his empty glass.

"Another margarita?" His voice was like gravel.

"You said one drink," she said softly, still not meeting his eyes.

"I'd hoped you might want another."

"No," she said. "Thank you for the offer, but no. I have a lot of work to get through tomorrow." Feeling like she needed to make the excuse stronger, she added, "Making last-minute arrangements for our trip to Sydney in a couple of weeks." They would look at potential retail space for one of their first brand-name stores, a companion to the Melbourne shop.

"I'm looking forward to it."

She stood, smoothing down her jacket with a trembling hand. "So, I'd better make it an early night."

He moved to her side and settled his palm into the small of her back. "I'll see you home."

Macy bit down on her lip. She needed this date over before she did something truly stupid—like press herself against him and wind her arms around his neck. "That won't be necessary."

He guided her through the room. "It'll be my pleasure. I've always seen my dates home."

Once they stood on the pavement, she turned to face him in the dappled streetlight. "No, really, I'm fine."

Ryder gave a half smile, as if he knew exactly what she was doing. "I won't compromise on this."

He picked up her hand and laid a soft kiss on her wrist that sent a slow burn through her bloodstream. She snatched her hand back—she couldn't let herself be dazzled.

Ryder gave another half smile. Then he turned to hail a cab. A bright orange car pulled up on the street in front of them and she slid into the backseat, soon joined by Ryder. He was close, so close, and it was much more intimate sharing the backseat of a sedan than in a public bar.

"Where to, Macy?" Ryder asked.

She clipped her seat belt, determined to keep her distance at all costs—a promotion was worth more than a night in the boss's bed.

Ryder listened to Macy give the driver her address and frowned. Having never been to Melbourne before, there were only a few streets that were familiar to his ears.

"You live next door to our office?"

She settled back into her seat. "Yes."

Though it would have been covered in her resume, he remembered the location of both her previous workplace and home address from the dossier he'd had prepared on her once he'd decided they would marry. And her home those three weeks ago was not their current destination.

He cocked his head on the side. "Your last job was on the other side of Melbourne."

"It was," she conceded, glancing at the city streets and the evening traffic through her window, before returning her gaze to him. "I moved."

Ryder adjusted his long legs to turn his frame more toward her. This little pearl of insight was too valuable to let pass. "You moved for a two-month project?"

She raised one shoulder and let it fall. "I like to be near my work."

Very near. "Do you always move when you change jobs?"

Macy shifted in her seat, not quite squirming, but definitely not happy answering the question. Interesting.

Then she called up another polite smile. "Usually. It makes sense to be near where I spend the majority of my day. And it means I can be called in on short notice."

He frowned, considering the pieces of the puzzle. There was more to it. "You live in temporary places."

She nodded once. "They suit my purposes."

They pulled up at the downtown high-rise apartment block and Ryder leaned forward to look at the building through the windscreen. "In what way?"

"They're temporary." Macy clasped the door handle. "Thanks for seeing me home."

He swiveled back to her. She thought he'd leave her alone on a city street? Not likely. Besides, it was time he put his proposition on the table. They'd made a connection—now he had to hope it was enough to back up the logic of his offer.

Ryder thrust some Australian notes at the driver. "I'm seeing you to your door."

Her lush lips compressed into a flat line. "There's no need. Really."

He took his change and thanked the driver. "Yes, there is."

She inclined her head, accepting graciously, if a little reluctantly.

Feeling upbeat, he stepped out onto the road and circled around to meet Macy on the pavement. It was a good sign she didn't have roots here. She wouldn't have trouble moving back to the States with him.

He laid a hand on the small of her back as they walked into the foyer of her building. Besides the doorman who stood discreetly at the entrance, they were alone, and the sounds of their shoes on the marble floors echoed through the softly lit interior.

Their first date had gone well, all things considered. Now he just needed to garner an invitation to her apartment and outline his offer and its merits.

Three steps into the silent foyer, Macy turned on the marble floor and faced him. "I only have to go up that elevator. You've seen me home." She moistened her lips and he couldn't have dragged his gaze away with a gun to his head. Her scent, something exotic, surrounded him.

She was so damn beautiful he had to replay her words in his head to get her meaning. Was it a good thing or bad that the woman he wanted to marry made his body overheat and frazzled his brain?

"Invite me up," he said.

She shivered almost imperceptibly, but then arched one eyebrow, as if in control. "Why would I do that?"

A slow smile spread across his face. Her veneer of control called to him, compelled him to move closer. He could see her writhing in his bed, in his arms, under him, all thoughts of control long gone.

His voice, when he found it, was rough. "There's something I want to talk to you about."

Macy glanced at his mouth then met his eyes. "I don't think talking's what you have in mind."

He reached and found her fingers with his, holding them at his side in the lightest of clasps. "Sure, just because I want to talk doesn't mean I'm not aching to touch you." *To kiss you. To taste you.*

Her pupils dilated to almost cover her hazel irises but she didn't move.

He leaned over and brushed his lips lightly across hers, meaning it to be no more than a peck, a brief demonstration of his words. He began to pull away but he couldn't help gently touching her mouth again. Those lips had been on his mind for twelve hours straight. Just one more touch…

Her mouth yielded, opened to him, and he needed no second invitation for something he'd been wanting to do since she'd arrived at the bar. As he deepened the kiss, he moved forward, closing the distance but not pressing against her—not yet—the bulk of his coat ensuring a respectable distance. Her tongue lightly touched his, a caress sweeter than he'd even imagined.

Drunk on her exotic scent, he lifted his hands to cup her face, finding her cheeks were like silk under his palms. He felt her hands on his shoulders, lightly, then more assured as they traveled an exquisite path to his neck before her fingers tangled in his hair. He was lost. He moved—

A flash went off, lighting up the room, and Ryder pulled back, blinking, scanning the area. Through the front glass wall, a lone photographer stood with a long lens zoom, still clicking and flashing rapidly. The doorman was already in action, racing to the photographer, and Ryder shoved Macy into an alcove where she'd be more protected, then stormed to the door. By the time he reached the spot, the photographer was running down the street.

The paparazzi had found him.

Breathing choppy, he narrowed his eyes and watched the coward flee. He'd managed to avoid them since landing in Australia. They targeted him every so often, but they'd stepped up their assault since his father's death—on him, and his half brothers Seth and Jesse. Most of the time he ignored them and didn't let the media affect his life, but they'd just interrupted a very private moment. One he was enjoying immensely. He kicked at the concrete path, accepted the apologies of the doorman, then strode back inside to find Macy.

She stood in the alcove, her arms hugging her waist, her face a shade paler than before. Without thinking, he wrapped his arms around her, attempting to take away the aftertaste of the shock. She must be more used to being photographed than him, but since he hadn't seen recent photos of her in the papers, it'd probably been a while for her. And they'd both been so carried away by that kiss, she was probably still reeling from its abrupt ending.

"I'm sorry," he whispered into her hair.

She stood motionless in his embrace, arms still around her own waist, a world away from him. "I think it was good timing," she said unsteadily.

"What do you mean?" He held her a little tighter, suspecting where she was going.

Disengaging herself from his arms, she stepped back. Her shoulders were square, ready to face whatever came, but her eyes were haunted. Ryder clenched his fists to stop from reaching for her again.

She took a deep breath and let it out in measured evenness. "I won't have an affair with my boss. I've spent too much time building my professional reputation to see it destroyed over a fling."

"What makes you think I'm only interested in a fling?"

Her eyes held a world of pain and cynicism. "Experience."

She'd been hurt. Thinking of her being hurt, betrayed, made him want to reach for her all the more, to offer words of comfort, but he knew she wouldn't want sympathy so he bit them back and waited.

She glanced at the spot where the intruder had been, then back to him. "I'm sorry, I never should have agreed to this date." She pulled herself up to her full height, spine stiff. "Thank you for the drink, but you have to realize we can't repeat it."

He frowned. This was clearly going to be a problem he'd need to overcome before he could convince her to marry him. Or, more pressingly, to kiss him again.

He needed to tread gently. Lifting her chin with a knuckle, he said, "Macy, don't let a parasite of a photographer ruin our night. We were enjoying ourselves until that flash went off."

Her eyes softened for a moment and he thought she was with him, but then her shutters came down.

"I—I have to go." She whirled and walked a little too fast toward the elevator. Jaw clenched, he watched her leave, telling himself not to follow, not to come on too strong and ruin this. No matter how much he wanted to go after her, comfort her, his whole future depended on not scaring her away.

When the elevator pinged and she disappeared behind mirrored doors, he was left alone. The empty feeling that over took him was strangely hard to swallow for a man who prided himself on being a loner. He just didn't want to leave this blasted foyer where they'd kissed only moments ago.

Don't be sentimental and stupid. Ryder turned and strode outside to find another cab.

Their wedding couldn't come soon enough.

Three

Macy stepped into the hall, letting the door to her serviced apartment click shut behind her. The night had been long and sleepless with images of Ryder replaying in her mind. His face so close as his mouth descended to hers…his short hair spiked between her fingers…his breath warming her cheeks…

Sensations from that kiss had tormented her body until the sheets had become a twisted mess and she'd had to trade any hopes of sleep for early morning coffee.

She pressed the elevator button and tapped the toe of her three-inch heels until the doors swished open. Facing him this morning would be difficult, knowing how she'd acted last night.

She'd kissed her boss.

Would he take her seriously in the office now?

Would he try to repeat the intimacy?

Would the other staff members be able to tell she'd

been kissed by the CEO of the company, and if so, would they snigger behind their hands thinking she'd tried to sleep her way to a promotion?

She'd worn pumps higher than the normal kitten heels she routinely wore to work to eliminate some of his height advantage, even though they'd still only bring her to his forehead or so. And she'd chosen a professional look—a duck-egg-blue silk blouse with a high collar and a fine wool skirt. She'd pulled her hair back tightly into a French twist to make sure she sent no sexual signals.

The kiss, bone-melting as it may have been, could not be repeated if she wanted to keep her reputation. Or her sanity.

As the elevator arrived at the ground floor, her phone rang. She flicked it open and thumbed the talk button.

Ryder's deep voice came down the line. "I can explain."

She smiled grimly. It was a little late, but at least it was a step in the right direction.

She waved to the doorman and stepped out onto the misty street. "I'd rather forget it. One kiss, it's over, we'll move on."

There was a pause on the line. "Have you read the papers?"

She pulled her scarf a bit tighter against the early morning chill. And frowned. "No."

"I'm on my way. I'll be at work in ten minutes."

The phone disconnected.

She threw it in her bag and walked just a little faster into the office building next door that housed the temporary Chocolate Diva suites.

He'd mentioned the papers. It could be something about the company's tentative plans to move into the Australian market. Or...it could be about the photographer last night.

He'd been at a distance and shooting through glass for the few seconds before Ryder had given chase. She'd hoped any shots he'd fired off would be unusable.

But either way—a company story or a paparazzi shot—why would Ryder need to explain?

Reaching her office door, she had to stop herself rushing as she booted up her computer and clicked on the link to the Melbourne papers.

And then her stomach dropped clear to her toes.

There on the *front page* was a shot of Ryder kissing her in the foyer of her apartment building. The photo was a little grainy but there was no doubt it was them. Her eyes flicked to the headline.

Bramson Buys Ashley Int. Heiress.

She read down, her breath coming a little faster with each line.

"...in a secret deal between Bramson and Ian Ashley..."

"...our source said off the record that Macy Ashley's hand in marriage was the price..."

"...Bramson wanted to marry the younger, prettier Ashley heiress but was told the only option was Macy..."

"...Bramson is believed to have completed the deal with Ms. Ashley last night..."

Macy's hand flew to her mouth as her body shook. Her brain screamed to turn off the screen but she couldn't look away.

It could all be lies.

Could be.

She bit down on her lip. He'd said on the phone he could explain.

She heard the elevator sound a second before Ryder strode into the office looking more like a commander on a battlefield—leading legions of men, his orders obeyed without question—than a man who'd come to apologize.

He pulled up in front of her desk and slid his hands into his pockets, making his charcoal suit jacket bunch above his wrists. She couldn't stand up—her knees may not have supported her weight—so she remained in her high-backed office chair.

Ryder looked down into her face, assessing. "You've read it."

Those were his first words? Not, *"It's a pack of lies"*? She leaned back into the executive chair, ready to be lied to. "Is it true?"

He drew in a deep breath and let it out slowly. "Some of it."

She focused on his burnt orange shirt with its neatly knotted charcoal tie as she took calming breaths. It was easier than looking into the eyes of yet another betrayer. "When were you going to tell me? Ever?"

"I intended to tell you last night," he said, his voice deep and rumbling.

She remembered him asking her to invite him up, that he had something important to say. She'd doubted him at the time, thinking he had something more physical on his mind. But it was possible he'd planned to explain this mess.

Slowly, she stood, stretching to her full height plus the three inches of her heels. "Which parts are true?"

He speared long fingers through his hair, held them there, then nodded before digging his hands into his pockets again. "I wanted to buy your father's company. He said he'd only sell to a son-in-law. Said it'd been a family company for three generations, and he intended that to continue into the fourth and fifth generations."

Bile rose in her throat. Yes, she could believe that of her father. It fitted his obsession with the future of his company, his total contempt for the idea that a *daughter* could be the one to hand it down to.

Her mouth twisted into a smile. "And apparently the deal on the table was only for me, much to your disappointment."

He held up a hand. "That part of the report was wrong. Your father's terms stipulated either daughter. I chose you."

Macy coughed out a laugh. She didn't believe that for a second. Kyla had always been the one the boys preferred—she was gorgeous, sexy and knew how to make a man come to her with her eyes. Of course Ryder would have chosen Kyla if he'd had the option.

Another thought struck. "Did you tell the media?"

"No." His forehead creased into a frown. "And to be honest, I can't think of how the media got hold of it. Surely your father wouldn't want this type of publicity, either?"

She sighed. "Kyla." It was her style.

"To jeopardize the sale?"

"To make me say no." And then land the bachelor catch of the year herself.

Which brought her back to the facts: her father had tried to sell her. And Ryder had jumped at the offer.

She looked out the window, down to the buildings below, before finding his eyes again. "I can't believe you even considered this, let alone agreed." She'd thought her ability to judge people had improved, but this demonstrated otherwise.

The elevator doors whooshed open out in the hall and she heard Tina dropping her bag on her desk outside.

Ryder didn't turn to the noise but he paused, waiting.

Tina poked her head around the door to give her usual morning greeting, but hesitated as she took in the scene. "Are you okay?"

Ryder didn't take his eyes off Macy as he replied. "We're fine. Shut the door on your way out."

Macy nodded to her assistant to confirm she was okay and Tina discreetly backed out, closing the door behind her.

As if they hadn't been interrupted, Ryder continued, his voice calm…persuasive. "We could have a good marriage. I'd be a faithful husband and an involved father with our children."

He'd already factored children into the equation? Macy blinked rapidly, trying to recapture her inner balance. This conversation became more bizarre with every passing minute.

With three easy steps he was behind the desk with her. Not within touching distance, but strategically eliminating the desk as a barrier.

"And I'm prepared to give you whatever you want. A house in Tuscany. Your own company. Diamonds, rubies, sapphires. Name your terms." He tilted his head to the side, the picture of reasonableness. "I think we'd get along well."

Macy crossed her arms under her breasts, needing some sort of protection. Not from his words, but from his presence. She could smell his scent and it brought back memories she couldn't afford to indulge right now.

She tilted her chin up. "I'm not sure where you got the idea that I'd be interested in your peculiar offer, but I will not now—nor will I ever—enter into a marriage of convenience. We don't know each other well enough to even have this conversation." She let her arms drop to her sides and let out a long breath. "What about love? Don't you want to wait and find a woman you love?"

Ryder rolled back his broad shoulders. "I have to be honest. Love isn't something I can offer."

Macy sucked in a breath at his quick and effortless dismissal of being able to love her. But it wasn't worth wasting energy over. She shook her head. "If you know anything about my family, you have to know the last man I'd ever marry is the one my father picked out for me."

His eyelids lowered a fraction as his voice became seductive. "You liked me last night."

Instinctively, she glanced at the screen on her desk, to the front page of the paper. To the image of Ryder kissing her. The shot had been taken as he cupped her cheeks with his hands, so they floated in the air, framing her face. Her throat went dry and she swallowed, remembering the crushing need she'd felt for him in that moment. Remembering the feel of him, the taste of him, the smell of him….

She ignored the ache that pressed in her chest, then, resolute, she looked up and met his eyes. "I won't break my contract—I'm a professional. I'll see out this project for the six weeks left. Then I'm gone. I don't want your promotion. And in the meantime, no more games. You'll keep your distance. There will be no meetings alone, or trips together like the one planned to Sydney in two weeks."

His shoulders squared and his feet moved a little wider apart. "Not acceptable."

She did a double take. "Pardon?"

"If you're seeing out the contract, then you still work for me. You will be on that plane to Sydney. I'm not going on an important trip with an accountant or a personal assistant when the team leader is available."

Macy took an unsteady step back, mind whirling. "You can't possibly expect—"

"I do." Any trace of the man who'd kissed her was gone from his expression as he cut her off. The Machine was back. "There are no lame ducks on my payroll. If you're staying, you'll carry out your duties properly."

He turned and strode out the door, leaving her open-mouthed, watching him.

Had she felt cornered before? Seemed she'd just discovered a whole new level of entrapment.

One week later, Macy stood in the foyer of her apartment building watching for Ryder's car. Right on the dot of 8:00 a.m. it arrived, yet she wasn't surprised. The Machine probably ran his whole life like clockwork.

The silver luxury car pulled to the curb and the uniformed driver circled to open her door. Macy smiled in greeting to Bernice in the front passenger seat. She'd worked with Ryder's personal assistant several times over the days the American team had been based in the Melbourne offices, and respected her.

"Thank you." She slid into the backseat where Ryder's solid length was settled.

"Good morning, Macy," he said, voice deep and rough. Dressed in a dark suit with a sky-blue shirt and tie the same shade, he dominated the sedan. His clean, woodsy scent filled the air.

She gave him a polite smile, belying the way the sight of him still made her pulse spike. "Good morning."

They'd kept the polite facade going since the morning the paparazzi photo had been in the paper. The way she wanted it. *Needed* it to keep her reaction to him under control.

As the driver climbed back behind the wheel and

pulled away, Ryder's voice rumbled again from beside her. "Bernice, did William send those updates?"

Pages rustled in the front and Ryder and his personal assistant were soon in deep conversation. With no desire to hear details of the U.S. operations of companies unrelated to her project, Macy blocked it out and thought about the delicate issue she needed to bring up with Ryder as soon as she got him alone.

From the day the paper ran the story about them, security guards had been stationed not only at the office, but also in front of her apartment building. When she left each night, the guards escorted her next door and shielded her from the small contingent of paparazzi that now staked out their street.

When she'd first quizzed her doorman about the guards at her apartment complex, he'd said the building's owner had employed them. But last night the doorman had let slip another piece of information that had confirmed her suspicions.

Ryder was behind the new security staff.

Macy bit down on her lip. Despite his cool, professional interactions with her in the past week, he'd acted—and was still acting—to keep her safe.

She'd been shocked, but her heart had melted a little at the revelation. No one had tried to safeguard her since the day her mother died. No one else had cared enough… until Ryder.

She took a deep breath and steadied herself as she reinforced the walls around her heart. Just because it seemed he'd been protecting her, she couldn't let herself be swayed into forgetting the deal he'd made with her father.

To buy her hand in marriage.

A secret transaction with her as the currency.

Suddenly there wasn't enough air in the car as her lungs struggled to inhale. She clicked the window control and when the breeze pushed gently against her face, she sucked in a deep breath.

"Are you all right?" Ryder asked, the palpable concern in his voice reaching across to caress her skin.

Macy almost laughed. He was at it again—making sure she was okay, when he was the cause of her problem. Confusing her.

She spared him a quick glance, nodded once to avoid further questions, then turned back to the safety of the window. The hairs at the back of her neck still prickled, and she knew he watched her.

While she focused on the passing scenery, Bernice's cheery voice caught her attention, asking questions about Melbourne.

Reluctantly, Macy closed the window and answered, keeping her eyes on the back of Bernice's head, trying in vain to be more focused on Bernice than the man mere inches from her on the backseat. *He'd betrayed her in a deal with her father.* Yet, in this moment, sitting beside him in the backseat of a car, all she could think of was the cab ride home seven days ago which had led to the bone-melting kiss in the lobby. A mere touching of lips that still kept her awake every night, tossing and turning.

Realizing her breaths were coming quicker, she dug out a report on the outer-Melbourne chocolate factory they were about to inspect with the view to purchase, and passed it to Ryder.

But he didn't raise a hand to take it. "I told you I'm not here to read reports. You can fill me in with a commentary during the tour."

Macy took it in her stride, and filed the report back into her briefcase. "Of course."

His BlackBerry beeped with a message, and as he thumbed the buttons, he asked, "How was the rest of your meeting with the ingredients supplier yesterday?"

She thought back to the afternoon meeting with a quick smile of satisfaction. "Very good. We nailed down the details on the points we'd discussed with you."

Ryder had been taking meetings all week with Australian, New Zealand and Southeast Asian managers from subsidiary companies of Bramson Food Holdings. Management from his biscuit company, prepackaged food company and sauce company had all been through the office yesterday for their chance to report in to the CEO.

In between his scheduled appointments, Ryder had made a point of keeping up with what was going on in her Chocolate Diva project.

He paused in his rapid one-handed typing on his BlackBerry and looked up at her. "Do you want to discuss any of it?"

She shook her head. "Thanks, but I'm happy with the progress."

When Ryder had started sitting in on her meetings, she'd been wary, feeling like Big Brother was watching over her shoulder. But as the days had passed, she'd found they worked well together as a team and had come to value his input.

He nodded approvingly and threw the BlackBerry on the seat beside him. "Good work."

They traveled in silence, Bernice and the driver chatting in quiet voices, Macy mentally running through the day's agenda and preparing the commentary she'd be giving Ryder at the factory.

And thinking about their upcoming conversation about her building's security.

Every so often, she flicked a glance at her boss lounging back in his seat. He occasionally watched the cityscape, but more often, made or took calls. Had his sleep been disturbed, too, or had the kiss been a purely clinical exercise for him with an eye on her father's company?

Even in the spacious luxury car, his legs lay spread to accommodate his considerable height, and one of his thighs rested within touching distance from hers. She could feel the body heat radiate across the distance, and she fought the urge to trail her fingers along the length to see if the muscles were as firm as they appeared through the taut fabric.

She turned to focus on the peak hour traffic on the motorway, unwilling to let herself indulge in fantasies of an incredibly inconvenient physical attraction. A man who treated her as a commodity to be bought and sold was not a man she could let herself lose control with again.

The problem was, she couldn't put Ryder in a simple box. Instead, when she thought about him she almost became dizzy from the back and forth….

He'd worked beside her in harmony for a week.

He'd tried to buy her in a business deal.

He was secretly protecting her from the media.

He wanted them to have a loveless marriage.

He brought her body to life like no man before.

Macy closed her eyes to quiet the tumult of emotions churning in her belly. This project would be over in one month and one week, and then she'd be free. Would never have to see Ryder Bramson again. And in ten days, Ryder would have finished his appointments with his management teams in the Asia-Pacific area and would be on a plane home to America.

All she had to do was survive ten days. The rest, after he was gone, would be easy.

Ten days.

She could do that.

She began reciting projected growth figures in her head and came very close to forgetting about the masculine thigh that lay mere inches from hers.

Very close, but not quite.

Four

After two hours of walking through the chocolate factory with Macy and shaking hands with employees, Ryder had developed a monster of a headache.

It was probably sleep deprivation—he'd had major trouble getting a full forty winks since the moment he'd kissed Macy's sweet lips. His body had been demanding a repeat performance, and more. Most nights he'd given up and worked until dawn…though he'd been tormented by visions of her mouth, the feel of her hands in his hair, the sensual sound she'd made in her throat when he'd claimed her lips.

As he strode down the corridor, he took a deep breath and brought his body back under control. He was dangerously close to showing everyone in the factory just how much he wanted her. Fatigue made restraint seem less appealing, despite knowing he had to take it slow with her.

He needed time to regroup. Mercifully, a twenty-minute break had been scheduled for him and Macy to discuss their thoughts so far.

The obsequious assistant manager who'd taken them on the morning's tour showed them into a boardroom. "This is where we'll be meeting with the factory's owner, so I thought you'd be most comfortable here. You won't have to move."

Macy shook his hand. "Thank you, Peter. We appreciate it."

Peter held her hand a moment too long and Ryder scowled. "I want a cup—no, make that a pot of coffee, a glass of water and a box of aspirin."

Macy disentangled her hand. "And a cup of Earl Grey tea, if you have it."

Peter hurried off to carry out his orders as Ryder stalked around the room, lowering the blinds to eliminate the curious stares from people walking past, then dimming the lights halfway for his headache's sake.

He turned to Macy, surveying her. She'd worn her silken hair back in a damn knot again. It'd been pulled back every time he'd seen her except the first day they'd met. And the night they'd kissed. The night he'd felt the long strands of her hair slide through his fingers.

He wondered how she'd react if he asked her to wear it down. Not well, judging by the thin frown line marring her forehead. She had something on her mind. He was sure no one else would have noticed but he'd spent almost a week watching her. And today she was a little distracted and that frown line appeared whenever she looked at him. It wouldn't be long before she told him what was bothering her.

He dug his hands into his pockets and rocked back on

his heels. "You handled that group of protesting workers well."

She lifted one shoulder and let it fall in an elegant shrug. "Their questions were reasonable."

"And yet you refused to answer those questions." Although the workers had barely realized that fact. She'd defused the tension effortlessly, leaving the workers feeling like they'd been heard as they returned to the production line.

Macy slid gracefully into a chair and laid her briefcase on the pale green table. "I'm in no position to promise them job security until we decide to buy the factory or not."

"Which only made it harder for you to find a response to placate them. Yet you did." He probably would have fobbed them off with a "no comment" so Macy's smooth handling of the situation impressed him all the more.

As Macy pulled her laptop from her briefcase, Ryder rubbed the tense muscles at the back of his neck. She obviously intended to use this session for work. Not going to happen. Not now that he finally had her alone again. Besides, he wanted to see if she'd tell him what was on her mind.

He undid his jacket buttons. "We don't need to go over those contracts, stats or whatever else you have in there. You've briefed me well enough during the tour and I'm confident in your knowledge if we move into other territory."

Macy hesitated then replaced her briefcase on the floor. "Okay." She turned alluring hazel eyes on him. "What do you want to do?"

He sank heavily into the chair at the head of the table just as a young woman entered with their drinks and a plate of sweets then discreetly slipped out again.

He popped two painkillers into his palm from the box on the tray. "We can sit in silence. Or we can talk. Your call." He swallowed the tablets then chased them down with the glass of water.

Macy shifted in her seat. "There is something I'd like to talk about."

He poured a black coffee and sat back, letting out a long breath. "Shoot."

He could almost see her change gears as she lifted her mug of tea to her lips and sipped. "You hired extra security for the front of the office building."

Ryder leaned his head against the padded headrest, warm mug nestled in his hands, and watched her. "I needed to. The paparazzi can't be trusted to abide by the law."

"And you instructed them to escort me home at night." Her voice was soft, almost musical. It soothed his aching head.

"It's only next door." It was his fault the vultures were following her. This was the least he could do.

She reached for a shortbread and held it between two slender fingers. "And I suspect you've told them to create diversions when I'm ready to go home. There tend to be fewer photographers when I step out than when I check through my office window."

"All part of the security firm's service." He lifted his legs onto the seat beside him and crossed them at the ankles.

In two delicate bites, she'd finished the sweet biscuit. Ryder swallowed hard. Oblivious to her effect on him—or was she?—Macy retrieved her tea. "Tell me another thing."

Drawing his focus from her mouth back to her dark-fringed eyes, he nodded.

"Are they the same firm supplying security to my apartment building?"

Her tone was polite inquisitiveness, but he sighed. Knowing where this was going, he casually took a slug of coffee before replying. "Yes."

"And you're paying for that service, as well." She cocked her head to the side and again he was reminded of her feline quality.

"Yes." Of course he'd made sure she was safe. What sort of reprobate would he be if he hadn't?

She picked up her mug again and held it in both hands as she sipped. "How did you convince the owner to let you do it? He apparently refused security once before because it would give the wrong image."

Ryder held back a smile. She missed nothing. In fact, he had the strongest feeling she saw far too much—she'd always keep him on his toes once they were married.

"I bought the building."

Macy's lightly glossed lips parted, as if to speak, then she closed them again. What emotion was she hiding behind her long lashes? Was she pleased he'd done it? Indifferent?

She crossed her legs and the higher foot began tapping a beat in the air. "Even if you'd signed a contract of sale, you wouldn't have ownership so soon."

"I overpaid for it and used cash to ensure immediate transfer of the deed." He'd paid through the nose, but it'd been worth it to have control over the building's security. To be able to safeguard Macy.

Her eyes flashed fire. "Ryder, I'm not some damsel you have to save. I can look after myself. I don't appreciate secret maneuverings in some misguided attempt to protect me."

He shrugged and threw back the rest of his coffee

before plonking the mug on the table. "It was no trouble." In truth, he'd been pleased to be able to do something for her.

"No trouble? You bought my building!" Seeing her exquisite mouth move with such passion was a pleasure to behold. He could have spent all day just watching it, just talking to her while she was fired up. But to be fair, he'd put her mind at ease.

"Macy, you agree the paparazzi problem was of my creation?"

Her eyes narrowed marginally and her answer was perfectly clear even before she replied. "Completely."

He arched a brow. "Then *allow* me to fix it."

She sucked in a lungful of air and held it for several beats. "On one condition."

"Name it."

"No more secret moves. If you do something for me or that affects me, then you tell me."

"Done." He dropped his feet to the ground and leaned over to her, hand outstretched.

She hesitated then shook on the deal. Her smooth skin against his sent a warm current of electricity rolling through his system. He didn't want to release her fingers, to lose the connection, and noticed she didn't let go, either. Her pupils slowly dilated. His senses became hyper-alert and his heart raced double-time. Every instinct he had screamed to lean over, pull her to him.

Before he could act there was a light knock on the door, and Macy quickly withdrew her hand.

The management team filed into the room and took seats, their faces serious at the prospect of a potential sale. But Ryder smiled inside. He'd already made a decision that was more important than anything that could come from this meeting.

He'd been biding his time for seven days, as he would for any business deal where the other person was skittish.

But that time was almost over. Macy had just shown she'd soon be ready for him to move their relationship forward. He had expected her to walk if she ever found out he'd bought her apartment building. She'd left her family behind once, and she was walking away from a promotion after this project was over. But she'd conceded on the building issue—it seemed she didn't mind his involvement in her life as much as she'd like him to think.

And her reaction to his touch spoke volumes.... He could still feel the effects sizzling through his bloodstream.

A little time to smooth things over after this and then he'd make a move.

Next step was to propose—properly this time. He'd do it in Sydney on their trip in one week.

He leaned back in his seat. Everything he wanted was nearly within his grasp.

Macy stood on the ground floor of their office building with a woman from another company, waiting for the lift, a small pile of folders in her arms. While the other woman chatted about the weather, Macy covertly scanned the buzz of people in the foyer for Ryder.

She'd successfully avoided being alone with him since the tour of the factory four days ago. Avoiding him was so much easier than saying no to him—something she knew she'd have to do soon though; Ryder Bramson wasn't a man to give up easily. She just hoped she had enough strength to do it when the time came, and not give in to her body's yearning.

When the lift arrived from the basement level, the doors slid open and she saw two of the American team. And Ryder. The man who still haunted her dreams and filled her unguarded thoughts. She took a deep breath and steadied herself against his magnetic pull.

Half a step behind the other woman, Macy entered and turned to face the doors, finding herself within touching distance beside her boss. Even without seeing him, she could feel his intoxicating presence, the primal masculinity that was barely hidden by the veneer of a businessman.

"Good morning, Macy."

"Hello, Mr. Bramson," she returned with as much formality and professionalism as she could muster.

From the corner of her eye, she saw him sink one hand into a trouser pocket. "Everything going well?"

She was uncomfortably aware of their audience—the others in the lift had no choice but to listen in. And since the morning of the photo in the paper, the staff had discreetly watched whenever she and Ryder crossed paths.

She wrapped her hands tightly around the folders in her hands and stood taller. "Everything is going very well, thank you."

They stopped at the first floor and the other woman waved goodbye and left. Macy held back a grimace. One less person acting as a buffer. The journey in the lift had never taken so long.

"The security staff aren't too intrusive?" Ryder asked casually. But she wasn't fooled—he was asking where they stood with their agreement that she'd accept his intervention on the security issue. She'd decided the day they'd discussed it at the factory that it was, in fact, his responsibility and it hadn't bothered her since.

"They've been very courteous and helpful."

"Good to hear," he said. "Tell me, how are things with my new acquisition?"

She felt the interest from their onlookers increase, felt their yearning to grasp the undercurrents of this conversation, their wondering if *she* was the acquisition. Ryder didn't seem to be bothered, but she wanted the rest of the staff to be clear on this point at least. "Everything seems fine with the building."

They finally reached their floor and the others filed away, but when she stepped out, Ryder placed a staying hand on her arm. He held her gaze for several seconds—though it seemed to be minutes—searching for something, asking a question. Then he drew in a long breath. "I'd like to see you in my office. How does twenty minutes from now suit?"

Her stomach fluttered and she wanted nothing more than to invent an excuse to avoid being alone with him. To avoid the conversation he planned on having—whatever it was, she was sure it wasn't about her project. It was personal, she knew that with everything inside her.

But despite all that had passed between them, he was still her boss, and a direct request was hard to deny.

"I'll be there." Gripping the folders tightly, and with head held high, she strode back to her office.

For twenty minutes, she distracted herself with work and determinedly ignored the mix of nerves and excitement in her belly. Then when the clock on her computer screen turned over to the appointed time, she stood and smoothed down her knee-length mocha skirt. She could handle whatever he said. Handle him. She'd survived worse.

She walked resolutely through the corridors, aware

her progress was being tracked by more than one person, and knocked on the closed door to Ryder's office.

"Come in," the gravelly voice beckoned from inside.

She opened the door and found him sitting at his desk, signing a pile of papers, each page in turn. He didn't look up. "Close the door and take a seat."

Visions of being alone with him suddenly filled her mind—in the cab on the night of their date; in the alcove of her apartment building where he'd kissed her—and her heart tripped over itself at the thought of being locked away with him again. But reason quickly took over. They were beyond that now. He'd laid his offer on the table and she'd refused. They were no more than employer and employee, and she'd ensure they stayed at that level.

She shut the door behind her.

Ryder still didn't look up as she sat in a chair that placed her directly opposite him. She crossed her legs. He continued to sign papers and move them to another pile. "I'll be with you in a moment. Bernice needs these for the courier who'll be here soon."

"That's fine." She watched him repeat the distinct signature over and over, noticing for the first time that he was writing with his left hand. She thought back and couldn't remember seeing him write before, but he'd both held and typed into his BlackBerry with his left hand.

Writing was a different animal though. There was something almost sexual about the way his square palm and long fingers curved around on the page as he signed his name, almost as if it were shaping her breast. Her breaths began to come a little faster. She'd never thought of left-handedness as being particular sexy, but on Ryder, something deep inside her wanted to reach out and grab him, link her fingers through his, bring them to her skin…

He dropped his pen and grabbed the completed pages, striking their ends against the desk to align them. The sharp noise brought her attention back to the office. Had she just been thinking they were like a regular employer and employee? She smothered a self-deprecating laugh.

He hit the intercom button on his phone and told Bernice the forms were ready, and within seconds, Bernice bustled in and took them, giving Macy a friendly greeting on her way out.

Ryder leaned back in his high-back chair and stretched his arms, which only served to highlight the breadth and muscularity of his shoulders. She took a deep breath and held it. She had to stop letting her mind drift to sexual thoughts about her boss. He was attractive, sure. Exceedingly. And he could kiss like the devil himself. But he wasn't like other men. He wanted her hand in marriage to buy a company. Things were far too complicated to let herself be sidetracked by attraction. The stakes were too high to let her guard down in case she found herself married to him before she realized it had happened. If anyone could do that to her, it would be this man.

He finished stretching and lifted his feet to rest his crossed ankles on the corner of his desk. "How are the plans for the trip to Sydney?"

"They're on track. I'd write you a report, but…"

"I wouldn't read it," he finished for her and smiled. "Macy, I know you were reluctant to take this trip with me, but I assure you, I'll be a perfect gentleman."

"I know you will," she admitted. She knew it was the truth—not that it would help with her own reactions.

"However," he said with a gleam in his eye, "if you change your mind during the trip, I'll be ready and waiting."

She hesitated, not quite trusting that gleam. One thing

wasn't in doubt—he had a remarkable ability to surprise her and she was quickly learning not to take anything at face value where her boss was concerned.

She cocked her head to the side and met his gaze. "Change my mind about marrying you?"

He shrugged one of his well-muscled shoulders. "That, or about your rule of keeping my distance. I'd be more than happy to repeat our date. Or," he said, voice deeper, "our kiss."

Images of that kiss came flooding back once more and filled her mind, her body, but she pushed them away and lifted her chin as she replied. "What would be the point of becoming involved when you want it to lead in a direction that I'll never go?"

"I can think of several reasons." His warm brown eyes smoldered. "Starting with how mind-blowing that kiss was."

It was as if champagne had been let loose in her bloodstream—despite her efforts to hold it back, now the effervescence flowed from her fingers to her toes and all the places in between. If he hadn't made that deal with her father, she could stop fighting and let their attraction take its natural course. But he had. And she couldn't give in. Once again she banked the fire that he so easily lit inside her and brought her body back under control.

That deal between Ryder and her father was creating grief on so many levels. She'd thought about it endlessly, and one thing still intrigued her.

She uncrossed her legs and sat a little straighter. "Will you tell me something?"

"Anything," he said, not bothering to hide that he was drawing his attention from her legs back to her face.

"You've put your wedding vows, *yourself* on the market

for the sake of your business, for money. Why would you let yourself be sold like that?"

His body snapped to attention. "Sold?"

"To get access to my father's company, you're willing to give up your chance to find a wife you love. Or—" she tapped a finger against her cheek "—are you thinking that our marriage would only last until the company is yours?"

He stood and moved to the front of his desk, leaning his weight back on it as he took her hands. His eyes—which only moments before had sizzled with sensual intent—were now serious. "Marriage vows are sacred. Once given they shouldn't be broken without a damn good reason."

She'd suspected he'd think that way after growing up with a father who hadn't taken his own vows seriously. Which made it all the more strange that he'd agreed to this plan.

She retracted her hands from his and stood, pacing to the other side of the room, giving herself a little distance so she could focus on the conversation, and not him. "You're willing to blow your chance of finding love. Blow it on me, and on getting that company?"

His shoulders went back and his brow furrowed. "That's not how I see it."

"Tell me then," she said, wanting to understand. Every time she unpeeled a layer, he showed her another, each one more intriguing than the last. "Explain how else this could be seen."

He took a deep breath and let it out slowly, as if steeling himself. "Love is not an option for me. I'm simply not put together that way."

He'd said something similar on the day he'd proposed, but she hadn't quite believed him. She could see now that he was very serious about it. What would make a man believe love wasn't an option for him? It had to be something buried deep. And, although he'd said he'd answer anything, to ask him *this* question felt like an invasion of his privacy. An intimacy too far.

Instead, she drifted back to stand beside her chair and stuck to the impact his belief about love had on their current situation. "So you'd always planned to marry without love."

He nodded. "Or not marry at all. But I'd prefer to marry, to have that companionship, children. A home. And when your father laid out his condition of sale, I have to admit, the thought of being married to you appealed, regardless of the business deal."

She felt her eyes widen. He really expected her to buy that? A stranger? He'd gone right past honesty, charm and believability and headed straight for trying to pull the wool over her eyes. He must think she was naive.

She arched an eyebrow. "Tell me how I could appeal when we'd never met?"

His gaze flicked from her lips to her eyes. "This might sound crazy, but whenever your photo is in the paper—usually old photos they recycle when there's a story on your mother or sister—" he paused to clear his throat "—something in your eyes always haunted me."

She blinked at him. That was the last thing she'd expected him to say. No, beyond last—it was preposterous. "From a photo?"

"Yes," he said with certainty.

Macy swallowed hard. It was true. She saw it in his every feature. Ryder, a man with the world at his feet, had been fascinated by an old photo of her. Her knees wobbled and she sank back down into the chair. It didn't make sense, yet his gaze was solemn.

She thought back to something else he'd said the day he proposed. "You really did choose to pursue me over my sister when you had the option?"

A deep frown line appeared between his brows. "I told you I did."

Yet, it'd been the day after she'd met him in person for the first time. "I didn't believe you," she admitted.

"I mightn't have given the full story at times, but I've never once said something to you that's untrue. I would never lie to you, Macy."

She felt her mouth curve in a cynical smile. "Although, in the time we've known each other, there have been quite a few instances when you haven't given me the full story. Buying my apartment block. Wanting to buy my father's company. I just wonder what other 'full stories' there are yet to come out."

His eyes seemed to pierce hers, but then Bernice knocked on the door and poked her head in. "Your next appointment is here," she said to Ryder.

He nodded. "I'll be right out."

Macy rose. "I'll leave you to your appointment."

As she turned to leave, he grasped her hand and his warmth flowed from his hand to hers, heating her body. "I meant what I said. About you changing your mind." His gaze came to rest on her lips. "Say the word, Macy."

Her skin prickled with unwanted heat. He was so close. His mouth was so close. She shut her eyes for a long moment against his power. Then she took a deliberate step back and he released her hand.

At the door she turned. "I appreciate the option. But we both know it will never happen."

Then she walked on unsteady legs back to her own office to focus on something besides her boss and the trip they were taking alone in only a few days.

Five

Macy swallowed away the tightness in her throat, clenched her fingers around her briefcase strap and stepped onto the chartered jet. Her fear of flying meant each plane trip was a leap of faith, but she would never give in and let anxiety rule her life. She was stronger than her fear.

Seeing Ryder up ahead, already settled into his spacious seat, she made her legs move and ignored the turmoil in her belly.

"Good morning, Macy," his deep voice rumbled.

"Good morning," she said through stiff lips.

His eyes changed, suddenly alert and focused. Had he guessed? The last person she wanted to know about her phobia was her boss. Between him being her employer, and her body's uncontrollable reaction to his, she already felt too vulnerable around him. Handing him knowledge of her weakness would be a step too far.

She stopped at a seat away from his and put her bag down to take off her coat. But Ryder indicated the seat beside him.

"Sit with me. You can brief me on what we'll see in Sydney."

Macy hesitated but covered her pause by folding her bulky jacket. If she sat beside him, she might be able to conceal her fear of flying for most of the trip, but the landing would be harder to bluff. She hated landings.

"I've already briefed you on the trip and I can't explain much more until we arrive in the shop space. Surely you'd like the time to catch up on reports from your other holdings?" She'd seen Bernice pack a pile of them in his briefcase.

Ryder stretched out in his seat, his long legs crossing at the ankles. "Why would I want to read reports about companies Bramson Holdings owns, when I can speak face-to-face about this one?"

Macy held back a sigh as she collected her bag and coat and moved across to the recliner seat beside him. She'd be fine. She'd covered her anxiety from the world for years, and no one had ever guessed. Why would Ryder be any different?

She settled in, buckling her seat belt firmly, then glanced across at her boss.

He watched her with his heavy-lidded gaze. "Tell me about your time in Melbourne."

His voice, so deep and resonant, seemed to travel through her body. She'd been trying not to let it affect her in the past week—an unrealistic goal at the best of times—but now he was so near, it felt as if his voice was caressing her skin, filling her senses, stirring her blood.

In an attempt to stem the tide, she blinked slowly. "There's nothing to tell."

He turned in his seat, squaring his shoulders to her, a teasing glint in his eye. "I can't believe there's nothing. You must have something you can tell me."

His body was close, so close, making her think of the night they kissed, and it made her a little light-headed. She could almost feel his hard chest under her palms again, his warm breath on her cheek.

She swallowed. "There is nothing about my life you would find interesting."

"I beg to differ." He folded his arms, waiting.

Her pulse picked up speed. How would he react if she leaned over and kissed him now? He hadn't tried to kiss her since the night in her building, but he'd made the offer in his office that he'd be ready and waiting if she changed her mind. And every so often she'd caught him looking at her. Perhaps he might return the kiss and she could sink into the heaven she'd found in his embrace….

He still sat with his arms crossed over his broad chest, waiting, but something in his expression changed. Deepened. As if he was reading her mind. Slowly, his arms unraveled and he reached across to smooth a wisp of hair that had escaped her French twist.

The breath stalled in her lungs. Her body heated. The feel of his hand finally making contact with her skin again—one simple touch—aroused her more than any other man could achieve with a concerted effort.

For one uninhibited, perfect moment, she leaned into his palm as it lingered on her cheek. She watched his pupils dilate and his chest expand with his indrawn breath.

Then she shored up all the willpower in her possession and moved away from his hand. Ryder Bramson was dangerously attractive. She wasn't the only one to notice—the tabloids loved to run pictures of him. What she felt wasn't anything more than what any woman would feel sitting beside him. And her father was counting on that to help him gain a son-in-law and sell his company.

Ryder must know his own appeal to women, too. And his plan mirrored her father's—he wanted her to marry him so he could buy Ashley International. He wouldn't be above using his appeal when the stakes were high.

Such a simple trap.

One she couldn't afford to fall into.

Heart still racing, Macy looked down at her lap, and smoothed her hands over her taupe linen trousers, ironing out the wrinkles from sitting. From the corner of her eye, she saw Ryder's hand drop and she fought with herself not to reach for it, to reach for *him*.

Without saying a word, he leaned back into his seat, looking out the window, just as the seat belt light went on and the copilot ducked his head out the door.

"We're ready for takeoff, Mr. Bramson."

"Thank you, Brent," Ryder replied.

Macy needed to get them back onto a professional footing. Needed to be able to talk to her boss without her imagination pulling her in futile directions.

She cleared her throat and grabbed the first topic that came to mind. "The retail space we'll be seeing has only recently come onto the market."

Ryder searched her face, his gaze resting on her mouth for a moment, then nodded. "Tell me why you think it's better for our needs than the others on your list."

Macy relaxed. She was back on solid ground—business. She could do this. Work side by side with a boss she was attracted to.

If she could just survive the plane trip without losing her head, she'd make it.

Ryder checked his watch. They'd be landing soon.

He'd had a fruitful discussion with Macy about potential policies and directions that Chocolate Diva Australia could take, but there had been something different about her. Something he couldn't quite put his finger on, but it was almost like she was on edge.

Had it just been from when he'd given into sweet temptation and smoothed her hair from her face, or was it more?

As they prepared to land, the seat belt sign lit up and Ryder buckled himself in. Macy had no need to—she'd been buckled in the whole journey—but she reached for the armrests. Her grip was a little tighter than necessary. Looking across at her, he saw the slightest tension in her jaw, the empty look in her eyes as she stared straight ahead. As if she was anxious but trying to cover it from him.

"Not fond of landings?" he asked.

She shrugged casually, belying the rigidity of her body. "They're not my favorite part of the flight."

She didn't elaborate, and knowing Macy she'd never admit a weakness. But her body language drew him in. "Had a bad experience with a landing?"

Her eyes flicked to his then back to the front. They were starting to slowly descend now and her knuckles whitened on the armrests. "No."

He placed his hand over hers and stroked the back with his fingers. Then something clicked in his brain. Her mother had been relatively famous, with her acting career just taking off, when she'd been killed in a plane crash.

He kicked himself for not thinking ahead and connecting the dots. For not realizing this could be hard for her.

The world had seen the images of the crumpled plane, had been flooded with photos of her mother on a movie set one week before her death, and had moved on. But this was Macy's private pain—completely removed from the public circus. He was almost reluctant to pry into something so personal. But another glance at her clenched hands and he knew he couldn't leave her as she was.

"Your mother?" he asked softly.

She nodded once, still staring ahead, her body radiating tension now—as if his insight had given her permission to feel the fear more fully.

He peeled her fingers from the armrest and gripped her hand tightly in his, his heart ripping open for the little girl whose mother hadn't come home. For the woman here and now. He wanted to shield her, gather her against him and tell her she'd be all right.

But he couldn't let her see that—his pity would only make her feel more vulnerable, a fate worse than death to Macy.

He cast around for a way to take her mind off the situation. Something…distracting. She desperately needed a life raft. No question, she'd hate grabbing onto it, but she needed one nonetheless. And he was the only one here.

He looked at the scenery out the window, and found an idea. "Have I told you about my ideal Australian holiday?"

Her eyes darted to his, confused, then back to the front of the plane.

"Obviously I've failed to mention it. Perhaps I'll get time for it after we've finished with the business from your project." He settled into his seat, bringing her hand—still wrapped in his—to lie on his thigh. He liked it there. "You might like to come with me. It starts with a field of grass surrounded by mountains."

Her eyes turned to him, lingered a moment this time, a corner of her mouth twitching before she returned her scrutiny ahead.

"We'll be there alone with a picnic basket. No one for hundreds of miles. The grass is peppered with bluebells and the sun is warm." He tried to assess her reaction. How thick should he lay it on? "Surrounding the field is a rainforest and—"

Without turning, she interrupted, a reluctant smile on her face. "What planet has rainforest and a field of grass with bluebells growing beside each other?"

Okay. Perhaps he'd gone too far. But at least she was smiling. "I said it was an *ideal* holiday, Macy. Work with me."

The tension in her shoulders relaxed a little. "Okay, keep going."

"As I said, we'll be alone and we'll run through the field toward the clear lake. When we reach it we strip off to our bathing suits and dive in."

"Do we check for crocodiles? Because if we're in the north of Australia where a lot of the rainforest is, I think we should check for crocodiles first." She faced him as she asked and the tension around her face had softened.

His chest swelled. It was working. He nudged a little closer and whispered, "There are no crocodiles in my lake. It's safe and the water's always warm."

"Good." Her hand released its death-grip on his to a more companionable clasp.

"We swim lazily until we've had enough." This near, he could smell the scent of her skin, wanted to lean across that last space separating them and kiss her neck. Instead, he sucked in a deep breath. "Then we drag ourselves from the water and lie on towels on the grass, letting the sun dry our skin."

The plane slowed for the final approach, engines straining and Macy jerked back into the tense position of earlier, her hand almost cutting off the blood supply in his.

"The setting looks good, but you look better in your bathing suit. It's red."

Ryder could see the battle in her body, between the fear and interest in his story. He decided to give his side an advantage over the enemy. Leaning that last inch, he whispered in her ear, "You roll over and run a hand down my bare back and I invite you onto my towel."

He felt it, he was winning—there was a change in the energy her body emitted.

"Do I go?" she breathed.

"You do. And you lie so close I can't think straight. All my mind registers is the feel of your body."

The plane's wheels hit the tarmac and the plane wobbled as it found its balance. Macy didn't jerk away, instead seeming to lean into him.

"I wrap my arms around you, wanting you so badly—"

Macy turned to claim his mouth as the plane raced along the tarmac, her tongue plunging in to meet his and he matched her move for move. He clasped her face with both hands, having turned himself on as much as her with his story.

He pulled at the pins in her hair and let it tumble gloriously down around his hands. The silken feel raised his blood pressure another notch.

He tasted her lips, her mouth, not able to get enough.

Both of them were jostled as the plane pulled up but he barely felt it. Barely noticed a thing other than Macy until the lights came back on and the door to the cockpit opened.

"Macy," he said against her lips. "We need to leave."

The fog of lust in her eyes gradually cleared and then she bit down on her swollen bottom lip.

"Thank you." She said it quietly, but the heartfelt meaning in the two words couldn't have been clearer.

"You're welcome." He stood and they both collected their carry-on luggage. He grabbed her hand and squeezed before they filed out of the plane and across the tarmac to their waiting limousine.

He knew she'd probably erect more barriers between them now he'd seen her vulnerable. But he'd be damned if he'd regret that kiss. It'd been incredible.

And he couldn't stop thinking about how to make it happen again.

The driver Macy had engaged for their trip dropped them in front of the shopping plaza downtown, then took their bags to the hotel. A dark car sent by the security firm Ryder hired in Melbourne had met them at the airport and now pulled over to let two men out. They stood on the pavement, a few feet away. Macy's shoulders tensed involuntarily, but she forced them to relax—far better to have the security there than not.

She edged closer to Ryder, amongst the people jostling and rushing, and pointed to the empty shop in front of them. "This is the one we've come to see."

Ryder lifted his sunglasses to the top of his head and stepped forward. "Main street, ground floor, corner with double frontage. Looks ideal."

The front was all glass, which would give great views

of the chocolate products, though it had been covered in newspaper from the inside so they couldn't see in.

A horn beeped in the traffic behind them, and Macy turned to the cars before Ryder's voice brought her attention back to him. "Is the agent meeting us here?"

"I had the driver pick up the key before meeting us, so we can just go in on our own." She withdrew the key from her briefcase and unlocked the door.

Ryder said a few words to the security then walked in behind her and shut the door. Abruptly, most of the sounds of the city cut off, as did the daylight. Crossing the room, she fumbled along the controls behind the counter until she found the light switches. She flicked them all on, drenching the room in bright neon lights.

She turned slowly, surveying a countertop that had been left by the previous tenant. It was an old wooden, carved bench. Unfortunately it would have to go—it didn't match the image they were after. All their fittings would be sleek glass and chrome. She ran a hand along the corner of the countertop, feeling its solidity. Its beauty of shape. A smile curved her lips—when she was running her own company, she'd have furnishings like this.

Another car horn outside made her look up, and she realized Ryder was at the edge of the room, leaning against a wall, hands in pockets, watching her. Even from six feet away, she could see his eyes were dark. And feel his heat.

She frowned and laid her briefcase on the counter. Keeping the image of a professional career woman was paramount when she was around him. Not giving him more openings to sway her to his plans of marriage and buying her father's company.

The kiss on the plane had been a mistake—she'd let her fear and vulnerability affect her actions. Though it had been incredibly sweet of Ryder to distract her with the story. She almost smiled at the memory, but stopped herself. He may have been sweet, but she couldn't forget his real agenda. A business marriage.

She stepped out from behind the counter and straightened her spine. "This is the front-runner of the retail spaces we've investigated, primarily for the location but it also has the floor space we need, and good access for regular deliveries."

Ryder pushed off the wall as if he'd never been staring at her and walked the floor, measuring by his stride. "It seems good. How's the price relative to similar properties?"

"More expensive than the others I short-listed, but when the extra features are taken into account, it's comparable."

Ryder continued pacing the room, assessing features as he went. "What length lease are they offering?"

"When I spoke to the agent, she—"

The door opened and a flash went off to her right, interrupting her sentence. Ryder swore and strode to the door, slammed it shut and locked it. Then he moved to a side wall and pulled back a corner of newspaper to look out.

A cold shiver ran across her skin. "Is it them?"

Without looking back, Ryder nodded. "About six paparazzi. It seems our supposed romance is still big news. Must be a slow news day in Sydney." He let out a disgusted snort then came to stand in front of her, hands on hips. "The security have moved them away from the door but they can't remove them completely from a public street. As I see it, you have two options."

"Go on." Despite the nausea in her belly, Macy blinked slowly, shoring up her reserves.

"One, we walk out the door, past the cameras to the hotel. The security will shield you from the worst of it and their car will meet us at the curb."

The room tilted. A vision of them pushing past the small throng, with repeated flashes going off, made her dizzy. She took a stiff breath. "I can do that. But I think I'll prefer option two."

"I ask the security to organize a diversion. We sit tight for half an hour to an hour, then we leave unnoticed."

Her stomach clenched. Memories surfaced of being with her mother, surrounded by paparazzi. Of being stalked by them after her mother's death, when she'd been hurting and confused and grieving.

Would he judge her for lacking fortitude? Would seeing her vulnerable twice in one day change the heat that had flared in his eyes a few moments ago? She knew he respected her professionally, and his opinion of her personally shouldn't matter, but the thought of losing his respect sent a hollowness to her stomach. "It seems the coward's way out."

"No." He dismissed her concern with a nonchalant shrug. "If they bother you, then why let them harass you when there's another option? All it will take is one call. We don't even have to open the door." He flipped open his cell phone. "Your decision."

She looked into Ryder's eyes, seeking, but his face was relaxed, genuinely offering her a choice. "Make the call." Relief surged through her veins as he dialed the number and made plans.

It shouldn't matter so much that people she didn't know would take her photo for other people she didn't know to look at in the papers. But it did. She'd always hated being put on display, but since her mother's death, the thought made her sick.

She heard Ryder ending his call and turned to see him pocketing his phone. "All done. Now we wait."

She nodded, acknowledging his words, but still uncomfortable that she'd needed him to organize the distraction. But, uncomfortable or not, he'd earned her gratitude. Again.

She took a breath, waited a beat, then met his eyes. "It means a lot to me that you've done this. Thank you."

He frowned. "If I wasn't here, they wouldn't be stalking you."

True, but the paparazzi were the real culprits. "Even so, you've been very tolerant and accommodating of my anxieties today."

He shrugged. "Everyone has fears."

She couldn't imagine Ryder Bramson fearing anything. He resembled an imposing warrior-leader from times past as much as the corporate giant he was.

Ryder's gut twisted as he saw the look in Macy's eye. He knew she was about to ask him about his own fears, and that was something he didn't talk about with anyone.

He turned, casting an arm out to encompass the site. And neatly changed the subject. "You've done well to find this place. In fact, you've done well in every facet of the job. I'd like you to rethink your plan to leave at the end of the project." *To leave him.*

She took the change in good grace, and her countenance changed to match. Smiling, she walked around the old counter and jumped up to perch on its edge.

She threw him a glance over her shoulder. "You know why I'm leaving. It has nothing to do with the job."

He followed her around to the other side of the counter and leaned a hip against its edge. "You made the decision when you were upset—"

She opened her mouth but he held up a hand.

"—and rightly so. There were things I should have told you up front, and I regret that. But we've moved past it. We could have a good working relationship if you take on the Australian arm of this company."

She smiled wryly, kicking her heels out straight ahead, her gaze focused on them. "You know, a month ago, I would have jumped at that offer. That job was everything I was working toward."

There was something in what she said—no, in what she wasn't saying—that drew him.

He folded his arms across his chest. "Why that job?"

She turned to smile up at him, eyes twinkling. "Shouldn't you be extolling the advantages of the position? Talking it up?"

"I'm curious." And he was. The drive to understand the mystery of Macy was stronger in this moment than any other concern. He could spend years asking her questions just to hear what she'd say. "There are hundreds of jobs that are suitable to your skills. Why is this one the one you wanted?"

Macy stilled. "Honestly?" she asked, her face candid, as if the enclosed room with its newspapered walls had become a haven away from the world. A place away from reality. He liked being there with her.

He swallowed. "Yes."

"I want to be CEO, so whether the company flourishes or perishes can be attributed to me and my team. I'd rather be CEO of a midsized company than have a senior position at a large company. And I want to be CEO of a company with an annual turnover in the range we forecast for Chocolate Diva."

"That's quite a specific aim."

She smiled again, acknowledging his point. "Yes, it is."

"Have you had that goal long?"

She breathed in slowly. Too slowly. "Eight years."

When he'd first met her, he'd found her hard to read—as he was sure she appeared to most people. But he was coming to understand the nuances of her expressions. Her gestures. The thought made his chest expand a fraction and drove him to try to understand what she was avoiding telling him.

"Why a company this size?"

She lifted one shoulder in a shrug. "It seemed a good number."

"No." He smiled lazily. "You haven't answered my question."

She arched an eyebrow, obviously a little surprised. "It's a good midsize company to prove myself in."

"Sounds reasonable." He pushed off the counter and moved to stand in front of her. "But that's not it. Why?"

She frowned at his rejection of her replies. "There's no other reason."

He leaned one hand on the countertop either side of her, trapping her and bringing their mouths within inches of each other. "Your eyes tell me there's more to this story," he murmured. "Why do you want a company this size, Macy?"

Silence met his question, but he waited. Her warm, sweet breath fanned over his face, driving him a little crazy, and still he waited.

Then she replied in a rush. "Because that's the size of my father's company."

It was the truth this time. He felt it in his bones. His fingers picked up a lock of hair that had escaped the confines of the twist she'd redone after their flight and toyed with it. "You want to beat him? Show you're better than him?"

Her pupils dilated as she looked from his eyes to his mouth. "No," she whispered.

"Tell me."

Her pink tongue slid across her lips then she closed her eyes, as if forming the thought in her mind. When she opened them again, she was bare, vulnerable. Willingly open to him. "I want to prove to him, and myself, that I should have been his heir. He wanted a son, but he didn't get one. And now he's willing to blackmail you into marrying me to keep the company in the family. It never entered his mind to pass it to me."

Ryder swore and shook his head at Ian Ashley's stupidity. He'd assumed Macy wasn't in line for the inheritance because she'd walked away from her family, not the other way around.

He picked up her hands, linking their fingers. "That's rough."

"You see my point?" She looked up at him, her wide hazel eyes searching his. She was extraordinarily pretty, but more than that pulled at him. It was as if he could see into her soul—see her need for someone to understand who she was and what she'd been through.

He squeezed her fingers. "Yes, I do. If it'd happened to me, I'd be more angry than you."

For a split second her eyes glistened. Then she blinked twice rapidly and disentangled their hands. When she met his eyes again, all traces of emotional vulnerability were gone.

She smiled. "Thanks."

Taking his cue from her, he stepped back, out of her personal space, but his mind couldn't make the same disconnect. He needed to do something. Something to make this right for her.

"Marry me, and after I buy your father's company, I'll put you in as CEO. You'll show everyone, including him, what a blazing good job you can do."

Her head tipped to the side and she frowned, as if surprised by his offer. But then she shook her head. "That's sweet, but no. I don't want his company anymore. It'd feel tainted."

"Okay then." He dug his hands into his pockets, mind racing, trying to find a solution for her, and solve his issue with his father's will at the same time. "How's this? Marry me and I'll give you a company twice the size of Ashley International. Lock, stock and barrel, it'll be yours."

She shook her head but smiled in acknowledgement of his offer as she refused it.

"You can have your career goal right now by marrying me." He arched a brow. "What's not to like?"

She crossed her trousered legs at the ankle, leaving her shiny black heels sitting in a sexy pose. "What meaning would it have if I don't earn it on my own?"

There was that integrity again. Damn, it was attractive. He was starting to think he'd want to marry this woman even without needing her father's company.

But his father's will—and it not leaving him a clear majority of stock—was still a factor. He needed to buy Ian Ashley's company and gain control of his board of directors. And he needed to marry Macy to buy it. He'd thought for a moment he'd found a way to entice her into the arrangement.

He'd just have to keep looking.

Three quick taps sounded on the door. The signal

from the security that all was clear and a car was waiting for them.

If only his marriage was as easy to arrange as fixing this paparazzi situation had been. But his plans for this afternoon and tonight should change her mind.

Six

They'd barely been in the limousine five minutes when Macy felt it slow to a stop. The security had called the limo back early and had been waiting to bundle them inside once the coast was clear. They now followed close behind. She checked out the window and saw the wide Opera House steps beneath its distinctive sails. "This is the wrong direction. The hotel's back in the city."

Ryder nodded to the driver and opened his door as he said over his shoulder. "There's something I want to do first."

She waited until he appeared to open her door, but didn't get out. "We have nothing on the schedule."

"This is a personal detour," he said as he offered her his hand.

Macy had never been a fan of detours from a set plan. Order and organization were the things that kept business and the world—including her life—operating smoothly.

But this was Ryder's business, therefore his call, so she took his hand and stepped from the limo.

Despite her ambivalence, one thing he'd said intrigued her. "Personal?"

He slipped his sunglasses from his jacket pocket, put them on and took in the expansive view. "I've never been to Sydney. My one previous Australian trip was also to Melbourne. There's something I'd like to see while I'm here."

Macy folded her arms under her breasts and studied his face. It didn't seem right—The Machine taking time out for sightseeing. She was sure his American staff would never believe her if she repeated the story.

She found her own sunglasses in her bag and slid them on. "I wouldn't have picked you for the tourist type."

He raised one eyebrow. "You weren't listening to my holiday description on the plane?"

She felt the heat rise up her chest and throat and turned away to the sails of the Opera House to obscure his view of her embarrassment. Except this wasn't simply embarrassment, the heat flowed through her veins to every square inch of skin. Her body was responding to the mere suggestion of his kiss, whether she wanted it to or not. And she hated that loss of control.

She tilted her chin up. "Ryder, I—"

"Before you say anything," he smoothly interjected, "I'll show you what I have in mind." He slipped an arm around her waist and gestured to the thirty-foot cruiser waiting at the jetty.

It was beautiful—large, sleek and white; its proud elegance easily outstripped the craft around it. But she'd be trapped alone with Ryder. Again. At the mercy of her own flawed ability to resist him. Again. The sweet pull of the heavenly and the allure of the dangerous had never been so strongly interlaced.

She took a small but symbolic step back from his arm. "I'm not sure we have time for a cruise. I have a lot of work to do at the hotel."

He dropped the arm she'd evaded and—seemingly unconcerned by her reluctance—dug both hands into his trouser pockets. "You have to eat, and lunch has been prepared for us on board. Think of it as your lunch break."

She looked at the gleaming cruiser. She'd never been out on the Harbour. Her trips to Sydney had always been quick business visits, but each time she'd promised herself that one day she'd explore this, the heart of Sydney. Maybe today was that day, and Ryder had handed her the opportunity. Could she do it? Ignore work for an hour or two, indulge herself, spend social time with her boss and not let it lead anywhere? She bit down on a secret smile, not willing to let it free, but ready to live in the moment for once.

A man in a white uniform waved to them from the cruiser and Ryder returned the greeting. She watched the exchange and suspicion pricked. "You already have a booking, don't you?"

He grinned in approval as he started walking her down to the jetty, obviously aware she'd made her decision. "I made it from Melbourne."

She shook her head as the smile she'd been restraining tried again to break free. Of course he had. This wasn't an unplanned detour—she'd just been unaware it was part of the schedule. Even the security men, leaning back against their car, seemed to know this was the next stop.

However, that didn't make her relax—now the question was, had he organized this to get her alone in a romantic setting? Or was it really just about him wanting a chance to see a world-famous landmark, the same way she'd been curious?

He guided her onto the cruiser and left her to speak to the captain. Macy looked around the Harbour, trying to sort out the competing thoughts tumbling around her head. She hadn't made much progress a few minutes later when she heard Ryder's footfalls on the deck come up behind her and then he joined her, leaning against the rail and looking over the view as the crew eased the boat out into the waterway. Despite being dressed in a handmade suit and polished shoes, he looked strangely at home. None of this made sense.

"What are you planning, Ryder?" she asked, an edge creeping into her voice.

"People talk about Sydney Harbour, they say it's beautiful. Some say the most beautiful harbor in the world." His sunglasses concealed his eyes but she could feel the truth in his words. "I've seen it on television, especially during the Sydney to Hobart yacht race, but I've never seen it in person."

The breeze fluttered around her as she leaned on the rail next to him, her head turned to watch the man beside her instead of the view he described. "You watch boat races?"

"Yacht races," he corrected, with a pained expression on his face. Then he flashed her a smile. "I learned to sail as a child, and always try to catch the best events. The America's Cup, Admiral's Cup, the Sydney to Hobart."

She tucked the strands of hair that had escaped her French knot behind her ears. Suddenly, she could see him on one of those yachts, commanding the crew to victory as effortlessly as he commanded his staff to financial success. Yet she suspected he usually didn't make time in his schedule for sailing or boat trips. And that he was granting her a rare insight into the inner sanctum of himself—he really did want to see Sydney Harbour on a boat.

Her heart relaxed its guard a little, honored that he'd wanted to share this with her. "This *is* all about you seeing an exquisite harbor, isn't it?"

One corner of his mouth kicked up. "If you get to see me away from the office for an hour and realize I'm not so bad, that wouldn't hurt, either."

She hesitated. Had she read the situation wrong? "You said you'd keep your distance. That you'd be a perfect gentleman on this trip." The kiss on the plane had already broken his rules, but she was positive he hadn't planned that. This cruise however…

"And I will be a gentleman." He laid a hand over his heart, the picture of innocence. "This is only lunch. On what's rumored to be the most spectacular harbor in the world."

The boat picked up speed a little and she leaned against the guardrail as she assessed his rugged features. "Nothing more?"

He clenched his hands around the waist-height metal bar, leaning out into the wind, his shirt billowing, his closely cropped hair tousled. Then he looked back, and even through his sunglasses she could tell his eyes were full of the devil. "Unless you ask."

"I won't," she said with certainty. It wasn't fair to give him mixed signals on this point.

He shrugged. "Then nothing more." He turned back to watch the water as it whipped past.

They traveled for a couple of minutes in companionable silence, only broken when Ryder pointed out Clark Island, one of the green bumps of land he said he recognized from watching Sydney Harbour on television. For a moment, Macy forgot about the undercurrents of their banter and was simply absorbed in sharing the beauty of her adopted country.

The steward emerged and handed them each a glass of champagne before showing them to a mammoth platter of tropical fruits and cheeses on the shaded upper deck.

Macy took her seat and eyed the mouthwatering choices, suddenly aware of how hungry she was. She took star fruit and an assortment of melon slices first, and as she sampled a sliver of honeydew melon, she realized Ryder was watching her. She stopped chewing and lowered the rest of the piece. "Is something wrong?"

"I'm watching you eat." He said the words innocently enough, but the heat in his eyes betrayed him.

A shiver of awareness erupted across her skin and she placed the melon on the plate. "You said you'd be a gentleman."

"I am. Mostly." He grinned and scooped a piece of honeydew from the platter for his own plate. "It's hard not to watch when you're enjoying your food so much. It's compelling. Sensual."

She refused to blush. Instead, she arched an eyebrow. "A gentleman wouldn't notice."

"A gentleman would have no blood in his veins not to notice your mouth and that fruit. But point taken." Within two bites he'd devoured his slice of melon. "Tell me, have you been on the Harbour before?"

Macy looked out across the blue, blue water. "No, I've never been to Sydney for more than a couple of days at a time."

"You've always worked in Melbourne?" He cut several wedges of brie, placed them on wholegrain crackers and put them on her plate before making some for himself.

She smiled her thanks and selected one as she spoke. "When I first moved to Australia, I studied for a business degree in Melbourne. Straight after I graduated, I took a six-month project in Brisbane."

"That's in the north?"

She nodded. "The capital of Queensland." It had been a great place to start her career—a city big enough to support large businesses, but small enough to make her mark. She'd had an apartment downtown that overlooked the botanical gardens, close to good eating places, and within walking distance to work. Just how she liked it.

"They have great beaches up there," Ryder said.

"So I've heard." Many of her colleagues had raved about their holidays on the coast either north or south of Brisbane. She took a bite of the creamy brie, then followed it with a sweet red grape.

He sipped his champagne and watched her over the rim. "You didn't see the beaches?"

"I'd just graduated." She shrugged one shoulder. "I couldn't afford to waste time."

"That's why weekends were invented," he said slowly.

"True." She nodded casually and popped a chunk of dragon fruit into her mouth. Some people may want to play at the end of the week, but weekends were perfect for making progress on deadlines and working from the comfort of home.

Ryder watched her for a moment longer, eyes narrowed. "You didn't take weekends, did you?"

"No," she admitted with a reluctant smile. He had a surprising ability to read her. It wasn't something she was used to—when she'd been younger, no one had watched her long enough, not with her mother or sister nearby. And once she'd struck out on her own, she'd quickly developed an aloof facade that had kept everyone at bay.

Everyone but this man.

Under the cover of taking lychees and cubes of matured cheese from the platter with the silver tongs, she observed him. Sunglasses hid his eyes as he slowly slid a piece of moist pawpaw past his lips. Her pulse spiked. Now she could see his point about watching someone eat fruit.

He blotted his mouth with the napkin then reached for the Swiss cheese. "Where else have you been?"

She pushed the lychees around her plate, bringing her pulse back under control. "I've flown into Perth a few times for meetings."

"And let me guess—" a teasing grin spread across his face "—all you saw was the inside of the car and a meeting room?"

"I did take in a couple of sunsets. It's on the west coast of Australia and the sunsets were spectacular. The best I've seen."

She found room for one final piece of kiwifruit, but then edged her plate away and wiped her fingers on her napkin.

"Had enough?" Ryder asked.

"Probably a little past enough, but the flavors were too tempting to leave."

He pushed back his chair and stood, then came around to pull her chair out. "Let's go back to the lower deck."

"You like being closer to the water," she guessed.

He rewarded her with a smile and held out an arm for her to lead the way. Once they were positioned again at the guardrail, where the wind danced through their hair and the smell of the sea was stronger, he turned to her. "Have you been to Tasmania?"

"Not had an opportunity."

"I'd like to go one day," he said, looking up to follow the path of a low-flying seagull.

Tasmania might have beautiful old growth rainforests and stunning mountains, but she knew the claim it would have on Ryder. "At the time of the Sydney to Hobart, I assume?"

"It'd be a sight to see, those yachts coming up Storm Bay." His voice was wistful and his gaze sought the yachts that dotted the Harbour. His staff might call him The Machine, but deep inside, something in Ryder didn't want to be a workaholic. It was as obvious as the bright sun in the sky that part of him wanted to stop and smell the roses. Or, more accurately, watch the yachts.

From observing her father, she knew that being a workaholic didn't bring joy, and she wanted happiness for Ryder.

"You should do it," she said softly. "Take some time for yourself and see the race firsthand."

His head whipped around to face her again, dark eyebrows raised. "Do you want to be the pot or the kettle in this scenario?"

Macy laughed and leaned her elbows on the rail, submitting herself to the breeze and the sound of the water rhythmically hitting the hull.

Time had flown by so quickly, she was surprised a few minutes later when they pulled back in to the jetty near the Opera House. She watched the crew work to secure the cruiser and felt an unwelcome pang of sadness that it was over already. Definitely time to switch back into work mode and leave the casualness of their "lunch break" behind.

She looked at Ryder who was watching the activity

of people on the shore. "Thank you," she said. "It was a memorable lunch."

He turned his back to the view and, after pushing his sunglasses to the top of his head, leaned his elbows on the rails behind him. "I hope memorable for more than the scenery."

She glanced at Ryder's profile. He looked better than any preened male model on a nautical photo shoot. The deck beneath her rocked with the movement of the water, but her legs fought more than the motion as they locked to avoid swaying. She clenched her jaw, her muscles, and brought her body back under control.

Then she tossed him the reply his comment deserved. "Are you fishing for a compliment, Mr. Bramson?"

A laugh seemed to roar up from his chest before he threw his head back and it erupted into the air around them. It took a few moments before he could reply. "Just wondering if my plan to get you to accept my proposal is moving forward."

The captain appeared and told them it was safe to disembark; Ryder thanked him and offered Macy his hand as they walked down the gangplank. Once they were on solid ground, she released his hand and headed for the waiting limousine. Ryder checked his long stride to fall into step beside her.

"Your plan?" she said, as they walked. "I think, instead of discussing your not-so-secret agenda to use me to buy a company, we should go back to the hotel so I can keep working on the job you pay me to do."

They reached the car, he opened the limousine door for her and offered his hand. "I can live with that. For now."

As he closed the door and circled the limo, Macy realized it was the *for now* that was the problem. He'd made his clearest signal yet that he hadn't given up. That he still intended to marry her.

The thought made her quiver.

Ryder stepped out of his shower and toweled off to the sound of the blues station he'd found on the hotel room radio. He'd told Macy to be ready at six because he was taking her out to dinner, but in truth, he'd organized a far more elaborate evening including a show at the Opera House, then a table at the city's most exclusive restaurant, followed by a walk along the moonlit Harbour shore.

And during the stroll, he'd propose properly.

She'd practically acknowledged this afternoon on the cruiser that they were compatible companions. And he had enormous respect and admiration for her—add that to the sexual heat they generated, and it was more than he'd expected to find in a wife. He had a good feeling about this marriage. She would, too, once he explained.

He pulled on boxers and black trousers, listening to the sounds of Macy's hairdryer in the second bedroom of their presidential suite. He paused by his open door, appreciating the intimacy of knowing his future wife was nearby, perhaps in a bathrobe. His blood heated and his body began its ascension to the aching need he always felt for her. He couldn't remember this desperate *wanting* with another woman. Usually, if a woman wasn't interested in a sexual relationship for whatever reason, he moved on, no harm, no foul. But not with Macy. Knowing she was in a bathroom on the other side of the wall was next to maddening.

His cell phone rang and he glanced around before remembering he'd left it on the coffee table in the sitting room. He strode out, not worried about his bare chest or feet since she was still busy in her bathroom.

Thumbing the button, he answered. "Bramson."

"Good evening, Mr. Bramson, it's Pia Baxter."

He greeted the executor of his father's estate as his gaze roamed to the door of Macy's room. What would she be wearing now? Would her body still be glistening with water from her shower?

"Mr. Bramson, I'm afraid I have some bad news."

Instantly, Ryder's attention was one hundred percent on the phone. He turned to face the wall of glass overlooking Sydney Harbour.

"Go on." He then realized this was an odd hour for someone in the U.S. to ring. Early morning, New York time. His spine stiffened.

"There's been an accident involving your half brother, Jesse Kentrell."

He sighed heavily. From what he knew of the spoiled brat, accidents weren't uncommon. Although...this must be bad to warrant a phone call to an estranged brother. Or perhaps it affected the will. "What sort of accident?"

"A car crash. I'm afraid he died at the scene."

For one awful moment, dark, clawing emotions rose in his chest, but without examining, or even naming them, he pushed them back down before they could affect him. They served no purpose; he'd learned that years ago. They only clouded judgment and distracted.

He heard Macy's door open but didn't turn, remaining focused on the information Pia Baxter was sharing. "Were others involved? Seth?"

"Seth Kentrell wasn't traveling with him. It was a single car accident and it seems Jesse was the driver. There was one passenger who was taken to hospital unconscious." Pia paused. "April Fairchild."

Ryder sucked in a breath. Jesse had dated minor celebrities in the past, but April Fairchild was the big leagues. America's favorite jazz singer was famous, talented, gorgeous…and unconscious. His stomach dipped as he comprehended the enormity of the situation.

"Is she seriously injured?" He felt Macy move behind him, standing only feet away.

"There's no word yet," Pia said. "I know you'll understand that neither her involvement nor her condition are public at this point."

"Of course. Thank you for informing me."

"Seth Kentrell's assistant asked me to pass the information to you. Mr. Kentrell feels that you might not have had a relationship with Jesse but he was still your brother and you deserve to know about his death before it hits the media."

Ryder swallowed past a ball of emotion in his throat. "Thank you, I appreciate it."

He disconnected and, holding any reaction the news had caused at bay, he turned to Macy.

She stood in a bronze satin sheath, feet bare, face free of makeup, hair up in another French twist. She was breathtaking. But her eyes were soft with concern. She must have realized something had happened from his comments or tone. She'd find out soon—the news would be everywhere by morning. He should leave it at that. But a tug deep in his chest drew him to share the information with her now. To seek her hand.

She offered it without hesitation, allowing him to interlace their fingers. And she waited in silence.

He cleared his throat. "My half brother—Jesse—has been killed."

"Oh, Ryder." She took a step in.

He stared at her fingers interlaced with his for a long

moment, then shook his head. "I met him twice, briefly. I didn't know him." *And now he never would.* His stomach hollowed.

Macy tugged on his fingers. "Come, sit down." She led him to an overstuffed gold brocade couch and he dropped heavily into its depths.

She sank down beside him, still holding his hand. "Did you want to know him?"

"No." He scrubbed his free hand through his hair. As a child he'd wished his brothers dead for the crime of stealing his father's love and attention. But that had been a hurt child lashing out—he couldn't ever reveal those feelings. Especially now that it'd happened. She'd think he was a monster.

"Will you go back for the funeral?"

Funeral? He hadn't thought that far ahead. "I don't know. The first time I was in the same place as Seth, Jesse and their mother all together was for my father's funeral a couple of months ago. I didn't acknowledge them."

He knew the ill feeling ran both ways, and was vaguely surprised Seth had asked his assistant to send word of Jesse's death. He and Seth had occasionally been at the same function or event, and through a mutual, silent understanding, neither had acknowledged the other. Except for once when an unknowing party guest had introduced them. He remembered the glacial indifference in Seth's eyes and knew his own stare would have been as brutally cold. They'd nodded once, then parted. No love lost, no common ground. Deep anger covered with a thick veneer of civility.

Macy squeezed his hand. "No matter what, he's your brother and you have a right to go to his funeral if you want."

"My brother," he repeated quietly. The word was

foreign on his lips. He'd never called him that before—had rarely referred to either Jesse or Seth in any way, but definitely not as "my brother."

"I was thirteen when my mother died." Macy's voice was gentle, but full of old pain. "I thought I'd die along with her, the ache was so bad."

He grasped her other hand, wishing he'd known her then to offer comfort. "I can't imagine."

The room receded then zoomed into hyper-focus as it hit him. He would never know his brother. Never form a relationship. His pulse raced, chest constricted. Never.

"Ryder?" He felt a soft hand on his forearm.

Blindly, he reached for that hand and brought it to his aching chest as if she could magically soothe the turmoil. He'd always thought of Jesse as a problem, an obstacle. One of the sons who'd taken his father's love and broken his family. But in some dark recess of his mind, he must have thought that one day they could meet properly, and…*something*. Not become best friends, but at least acknowledge each other. Perhaps even become acquaintances who met once a year to share a bottle of wine. Or *something…*

A yawning raw hole seemed to open within his chest and for a moment, the power of it paralyzed him. He fought against it, unwilling to give in to the dark emotions that wanted to claim his heart. He emerged victorious, but engulfed by a desperate need to fill the void.

Suddenly he was aware that Macy's arms were around him. He drew her closer, welcoming the comfort of human touch. Of *her* touch.

She stroked his back and his eyes drifted shut, absorbing the full extent of the sensation. Lifting her, he brought her to his lap, reveling in having her this near. He'd needed her touching him again since their first kiss in her lobby. But the kiss on the jet this morning had raised that need to a new peak.

He held her tight and, mercifully, she held him, too. She sat there, in his lap, letting him hold her for what seemed like an eternity. Until the thoughts of Jesse began to fade, and thoughts of Macy were all that filled his mind. And that desperate sense of need. He reached to pull the pins from that blasted French twist and growled in satisfaction as her gorgeous hair tumbled down.

He leaned his face into her neck, smelling her floral shampoo, the scent of her skin. "So beautiful," he whispered against her hair.

She turned away, as if she was unsure of what was happening between them. If it was right. *He* was sure. He used a knuckle to bring her face around and met her lips with his own. At first she didn't respond, and he coaxed, gently, knowing the passion that had been in her kiss on the plane. She might want to deny it but he knew he could rouse passion in her. Passion for him.

As his thumbs stroked her cheeks, he sucked her bottom lip into his mouth, biting softly, then ran his tongue along her top lip. She relaxed into him, moaning deep in her throat as his mouth moved over hers with all the desperation he felt. Heat seared his chest as her hands tentatively made contact with his naked skin, skimming across and up, over his shoulders. The touch was a flame to tinder—he'd dreamed of having her here but the reality would surely set him alight.

She twisted in his lap, reaching to touch more, and the pressure on his groin made him groan. He traced a path down her back, feeling the shape of her through the thin satin fabric. He felt until he found the zipper and tugged until the cap sleeves loosened enough for him to push them down, revealing her golden shoulder. Nothing could have stopped him from kissing the smooth perfection of her exposed skin.

She smelled like jasmine. The tang from her soap was erotic and he nipped, then kissed more skin, faster. He needed to taste all of her. His kisses moved back to her throat, desire for her pulsing through his entire body.

He found her mouth again, and the touch of her tongue on his, her tongue in his mouth, almost made him lose control. He scooped his hands under her knees, readying to carry her to his bed, where he could have unfettered access to all of her.

Hands on his shoulders, Macy pulled back, her chest rising and falling rapidly. "Ryder, I'm not sure about this. You're upset after the phone call." She laid a palm on his cheek. "This isn't the best time for either of us."

He heaved in a breath, willing his mind to work. There was a tiny frown line between her eyebrows, but her pupils were dilated and her skin was flushed. She desired him, that much was obvious. She just needed to know he wasn't using her to forget about his brother. Nothing could be further from the truth.

"Macy, I need you," he rasped. "I've craved you since that first day." He kissed the lobe of her ear, then whispered in her ear, "Tell me you need me as much. Please."

Her head rolled to one side, giving him easier access to her lobe. "I want you more than I've ever wanted anyone. More than I thought I *could* want anyone."

"Then forget everything else. Forget Ashley International and Chocolate Diva. Forget your father and my brother. This is just between you and me." He stood, taking her with him and setting her on her feet before holding out his hand.

"Come with me." He didn't intend their first time to

be on a couch—it would be in a bed, where he had the room to savor her properly. Where they could wake up tomorrow morning together.

He looked into her eyes, not hiding the need he had for her in this moment. In every moment. "Come with me, Macy."

She took a ragged breath and her luscious lips parted, as if to speak. Then she smiled, almost shyly, and took his outstretched hand.

Seven

Ryder pulled her to him, then crossed the vast sitting room, keeping her firmly pinned to his side. Macy's stomach quivered with anticipation. She'd never felt anything like this intoxicating mix of excitement and impatience, not even on Christmas Eve as a child, knowing there would be extravagant presents under the tree. The prospect of unwrapping Ryder surpassed any gift she could imagine.

She'd been resisting him for weeks, then when he'd had the call about his brother, her heart had gone out to him. And once she was beside him on the couch, his magnificent chest bare, him gripping her for dear life, she knew the resistance she'd been clinging to had been shattered. She'd tried to bolster it again when he'd kissed her, tried to hold the fraying edges of her self-restraint, but she'd been *yearning* for his kiss, dreaming of it at night and so reason had fled within minutes. It was one thing to withstand her attraction to him from across an office, or standing near him on a cruiser. It was quite another when they were alone on a couch and she was in his arms, feeling his body heat, smelling the masculine scent of his naked skin.

Since the night he'd kissed her in the lobby of her apartment building she'd been actively holding him at bay, now she'd reached the limits of her capacity to withstand the attraction. And in this moment she couldn't remember why she'd resisted so long.

At his room, Ryder caught her up against the door-frame. "I can't wait. It's a long trip to the bed." He lowered his mouth to hers, opening her lips in one smooth stroke. She clung to his shoulders, melting, dissolving into him. An earthy blues tune played in the background.

He arched back, breathing heavily, eyes almost black with desire. "I want to savor every single second."

He lifted her into the cradle of his arms and strode through the door. She'd never considered herself the being-carried-to-the-bed type, but the sheer masculinity of the action made her belly flutter, so she clung to his neck and surrendered to the experience.

He laid her carefully on the huge bed, draped in a burgundy cover and pillows. To her sensitized skin, the cool, crisp bedcover felt glorious, and she glided the back of her hands along the surface for the simple pleasure of it. Being here with Ryder was giving her permission to indulge her body's senses in a way she'd never allowed herself before. She'd been raised to be in control at all times, to always suspect the media was watching, and that had carried over into every aspect of her life. Ryder was stripping down those restraints. But she didn't question it; she'd think about it later.

He straightened and her breath faltered at the sight of

his muscled chest and shoulders. When he moved to join her on the bed, she held up a hand.

"Wait. You said you wanted to savor this and so do I." Emboldened by her awakening sensuousness, she took a shuddering breath. "Take off your trousers."

A trace of surprise flickered in his darkened eyes before he raised a brow in appreciation and smiled.

She swallowed and nodded. "I want to see you. Once you're down here I won't be able to see you like this."

Ryder unzipped the black pants with excruciating slowness, then let them slither down his strong, tanned thighs to the floor before stepping out. Restless on the bed, she wasn't sure this was the best way to be doing this—not touching for the seconds, minutes their bodies had been apart was making her tremble.

He rested his hands on hips above his black designer boxer shorts. "Shall I join you?" His voice was deep and husky and she took three heartbeats to respond.

"When you finish the job." She only just managed to push the words out, her throat was so tight.

Ryder cocked an eyebrow and held her gaze as he slid the boxer shorts down. For half their journey, Macy kept her eyes on his, but when she couldn't hold back any longer, she glanced down his chest, down his full length. Light played over firm muscle definition, robbing her of thought and breath.

A physique like that deserved appreciation. It deserved worship.

Want was such a weak word. If she didn't have him soon, she'd explode. She held an arm out to him and he came to her, kneeling up on the bed, moving closer until he hovered over her without touching. "Your turn."

"I can't with you there." She'd need more room

than he'd allowed her to take off the formfitting sheath dress.

"Try."

Macy smiled as she arched to reach behind and lower the zipper all the way down her back, pulling one arm from the sleeve. She brushed him accidentally as she maneuvered and Ryder claimed her mouth.

The other sleeve forgotten, she drew him down, kissing him back with more passion than she knew she possessed. Her heart soared—the only time she remembered feeling this *right* was the last time Ryder had kissed her.

His hips lay over hers and she groaned. "Ryder, I don't know how much longer I can wait."

"You'll just have to last, because I want this to go on all night." He straightened back onto his knees, one on each side of her thighs. "The rest of the dress needs to go."

She lifted and pulled her other arm from the sleeve, then sat up to pull the sheath over her head. What had been mere anticipation was building to fever pitch inside every cell of her body, and they'd barely done more than kiss. Though, she'd been fantasizing about this since he'd kissed her the night in her apartment's lobby. Had craved him since then.

He quickly disposed of her bra and panties, then his fingers lightly traced circles on her stomach and she shivered.

His eyes blazed. "You're exquisite."

Almost writhing with need, Macy reached for him, and he dragged her close. "I think about you all the time," he whispered.

He thought of marrying her. Her heart twisted a little, but she ignored it. He'd said tonight was just about them, not about her work on the project or him buying her father's company. And he was right. She pushed away everything in her mind but him and raised her mouth to his and hovered. "Kiss me."

"My absolute pleasure," he said as his head angled down. His tongue slipped inside her mouth and her lips caught it. She sucked, gently at first, but as his hips bucked against hers, she applied more pressure until he moaned, his body pressing along hers with delicious pressure. Her heart pounded, her need for him growing to epic proportions—beyond anything she'd experienced, so intense it would have scared her had it been anyone by Ryder. He somehow made her feel safe and out of control at the same time.

His mouth wrenched away and he trailed wet kisses down her throat to her breast, sucking, grazing his teeth over the tip. Her body contracted, muscles pulling tight. Thoughts could barely form in her mind, her entire world was the feel of him, the clean, musky scent of him.

Her hands found his buttocks, her nails scraping across the perfectly formed roundness.

"Ryder, now. Please."

He slithered down her body, his hands spanning her hips and plunged his tongue into her. Macy cried out. She looked down her body and met his eyes of dark chocolate. And then his tongue plunged again and this time it stayed, flicking rhythmically against her and the only sensation in the world was his warm mouth until she burst free, calling his name, unable to contain it, and then went limp against the bedcover.

She felt Ryder move back up her body, his breath almost as fast as hers. "Damn, you drive me crazy." His voice sounded ragged and, eyes still shut, she instinctively reached between their bodies to find him. When she did, she grasped him firmly. He was hot and solid in her palm and as she moved her fingers, he rasped, "Macy, I need to be inside you. I want to be as close as I can."

Her eyes flew open, body instantly alert again. "I want that, too." She rubbed him again with her fingertips.

"Then you'll have to stop that. I've been on a knife's edge since that plane ride this morning."

Her blood heated again and she reluctantly released him, squirming inside as the need rebuilt.

"Macy, I wanted this to last so much longer, but I can't. I'm having trouble lasting another second."

She kissed his salty chest. "It's perfect timing."

His pec muscles flexed as her tongue traced their contours and he moaned. Then he rolled away, off the bed, rummaged through his things, and retrieved a condom. In a flash, he'd sheathed himself and was back.

He moved over her, holding his weight on arms positioned on either side of her. She reached up to kiss him hungrily, wrapping her legs around his waist, inviting. As he surged forward, joining them, she linked one ankle over the other behind his back and held him there, relishing the pure intimacy of it.

When he pulled back, she lessened her grip and gave herself over to the surging rhythms. He kissed her and she clung to his shoulders, etching this feeling, the scents, his labored breathing into her mind, knowing she'd remember this moment until the day she died. If they never had more than this night, she'd own one dazzling memory of nirvana.

She flew higher, Ryder's intense gaze on her face driving her higher still, the slow, sexy croon from the radio rolling and swelling in flawless timing with the build of sensation within her, providing the soundtrack for a moment of perfection. Then mounting waves sent from heaven crashed through her body, dragging him with her. He groaned and murmured her name over and over, his voice a spent whisper warming her hair.

He rested his forehead against her and even at this close range she saw a lazy grin spread across his face.

"What?" she asked, still breathless.

"That was the most explosive experience of my life." He lifted his weight from her, moving to lie beside her.

Already missing his warmth and skin, Macy rolled toward him to reconnect. He scooped her in alongside him as a blues singer serenaded in the background.

She smiled into his shoulder, her leg draped across his. "I don't think I'll ever feel the same about the blues again."

Though in actuality, she knew she'd never feel the same about *herself* again…or Ryder. The thought sent a shiver down her spine so she pushed it away and snuggled in closer to the man who'd just taken her to unimaginable heights.

Macy woke in Ryder's hotel bed, with a lazy smile on her face. He was asleep beside her on his stomach, one arm above his head, wrapped around his pillow, the other proprietarily flung across her waist. Her skin under his hand was warmed by his body heat.

She started at the almost unbearable beauty of his back laid out before her. His shoulders were so broad, and in sleep, his muscle bulk was smooth and relaxed under his tan skin.

She ran a light hand along his shoulder blades, not wanting to wake him, but compelled to feel that magnificence, make sure it was real.

He stirred and opened his eyes. A smile spread slowly across his face. "That beats my alarm clock," he said, voice husky and deep from sleep.

She withdrew her hand, unsure of their relationship now. How do you address your boss when you wake in his bed after a night of pleasure beyond imagining?

He reached for her hand and interlaced their fingers. "Regrets?"

She rolled up onto an elbow, scrutinizing his face for cues. His features were open and relaxed, so she answered honestly. "Not unless you have any. You were upset, and—"

"Shh." He cupped her cheek with his warm palm. "This wasn't about my brother. The call hit me, sure. But I've been wanting you here so badly I haven't been sleeping."

She looked around the hotel room with an arched eyebrow. "You wanted me *here*?"

"It's a bed." He grinned. "I'm not fussy on the details." His face sobered. "Though I had planned on taking you out last night and impressing you with a romantic dinner—and I'll still do it one night soon. You deserve to be wined and dined."

She lay back down beside him, not wanting to break the magic, but knowing she had to. "You need to think about your brother. The funeral will be soon and, considering the flight back to the U.S., you'll need to leave right away if you want to go."

He shrugged a shoulder. "I don't think I will go. It'd be hypocritical. And it'd start a media frenzy which would impact on my mother."

She could understand wanting to avoid a media frenzy, especially about something as private as grief. "What about your other brother."

"Seth." Ryder frowned. "What about him?"

"Should you send him a message or something?"

"I don't know." He scrubbed a hand across his face. "We're in the middle of something...awkward."

The tightness in his voice jumped out and caught her attention. This was important. "What is it?"

He rolled onto his back and threw a hooked arm over his head. "My father's will split his majority share holdings between us, leaving no one in control. Effectively pitting us against each other."

"Oh, Ryder, that's horrible." She laid her fingertips on his cheek. "Why would he do that?"

He glanced over and gave her a humorless smile. "He was trying to help us get along."

"How would that make you get along?"

"I suppose he thought we'd suddenly become best friends, form a voting block and run the company cooperatively."

Macy shook her head at Warner Bramson's ignorance about his sons' personalities. Or had it been a last-minute attempt to heal the divide between his families? Either way, even she could see it would never work with a son used to being in control like Ryder. Or Seth, from what she'd read of him in the papers.

"What will you do?"

"Obtain a majority in my own right." His jaw was set. That was obviously nonnegotiable for him.

Suddenly, everything became crystal clear. She swallowed. "That's why you want to buy my father's company. It has some stock in Bramson Holdings."

He looked at her warily. "Yes."

"And to buy it, you need to marry me."

"Yes." He turned onto his side, eyes sharply focused on hers.

Her lungs felt constricted, working too fast, too

shallow. "I thought I was your key to buying a company, but it's so much more than that, isn't it?"

He nodded while reaching for her, as if afraid she'd pull away. Well, he was right about that. She sat up, taking the sheet with her and tucking it under her arms. She'd known he was after her for her father's company, but this was bigger…and felt grubbier somehow.

"Did you even want the project to go ahead? Or was it simply bait for me? Tell me I haven't been wasting all that time on a sham."

"It was part of my forward planning," he said, slowly, diplomatically. "I just bumped it up in the schedule to employ you. If you'd left the project, I'd still have employed someone else to finish it."

She dragged in a shaky breath. "But starting it now, this business trip to check on it, the marriage proposal, even this—" she waved an arm at his rumpled bed "—it's all to secure your father's company. It must mean a lot to you."

He sat bolt upright, eyes wide and serious. "Not this. I told you this is between you and me and I meant it. A separate issue."

She hesitated at the sincerity in his expression, but the turmoil deep in her chest spoke louder. "How can sex be a separate issue from a marriage proposal?"

"I don't know. It just is." He blew out a frustrated breath. "All I can tell you is that I want to marry you so I can get control of the company that should have been mine, but I want you in my bed again because every moment I'm not touching you is painful. My body goes into withdrawal and I ache to feel your skin, to kiss your mouth, to hold you against me."

She felt tears threatening but whether they were tears of frustration, betrayal or because his words moved her, she had no idea. It was as if the hotel room walls were moving in, pushing against her, robbing her of oxygen.

She stood, letting the sheet drop, heading for the door. "I need some space to breathe."

"Where are you going?" he asked, voice gravelly with concern.

She stopped at the door and turned, unworried that she was naked in front of him. Her emotional nakedness was much more disturbing than the physical. "For a walk."

He held up a finger and reached for his cell phone on the table beside the bed before dialing quickly. "It's Bramson. What's the situation outside? I see. Thank you." He hung up and stood. "The security firm says there are photographers outside the hotel waiting. My men can escort you on a walk if you'd like."

Walls everywhere were closing in on her. Even outside this room, outside the hotel. Tears threatened again, but she'd never let them spill over. She reached for a bathrobe hanging on a hook beside his bathroom to give herself something to do, and tugged the cord tight until she felt the burn on her skin. It didn't help. Her head still pounded, her lungs still struggled.

She looked back at Ryder, standing motionless, waiting for her reaction. His large, solid body called to her—invited her to fall into him, let him wrap his arms around her and provide comfort, make everything else go away. But that's how all this mess had started. Her attraction to him on the first day he'd walked into her offices. She'd been lost from that moment. And yet, he'd planned it....

She took a step closer to him, arms crossed tightly over her robe. "You did this. You came here to charm me into marriage, to get your father's company. You brought the media with you." She kept absolute control over her voice, not letting it rise the way it wanted to. "And now I can't walk outside. You've upended my life."

His face twisted, eyes tormented. "I never intended this. I thought it would be simpler."

The words hit her like a glass of cold water and she stumbled back before catching herself. "You thought I'd give in sooner? Fall at your feet?"

His face turned harsh as he shook his head. "You're twisting my words. I meant I didn't think the media would stalk us."

"Well, they are." She pulled the sides of the robe more firmly together. "And now I can't go for a run to get the space I need from what you've put in motion by coming here." She stalked back to the door.

"Where are you going?" he repeated his earlier question, but this time his tone was more commanding.

"Don't worry, I won't leave the building," she said as she shut the door behind her and headed for her room to get changed.

Ryder gave her two hours to work off her anger and confusion. He hated cooling his heels in the suite, but couldn't deny she had a right to her annoyance. It'd only been two weeks since he'd arrived, after all, and a lot had happened in that time. The paparazzi stalking her after a three-year break, finding out her hand in marriage was a clause in her father's sales contract, Ryder arriving and now explaining his own inheritance issues, her giving up on her goal of running Chocolate Diva Australia, and now their intimate relationship.

Two hours was the least he could give her to assimilate. He should probably give her more. But he couldn't tamp down his need to be there for her, to help her adjust to the changes, to see if he could help. To just be with her.

After checking the bar, he headed for the gym. He found her alone in the expansive room, on the treadmill, skin flushed deep pink, hair in a damp ponytail, workout clothes stuck to her body. Heat flared through his bloodstream, imagining her panting this way in his bed. For him. One night was nowhere near enough.

She looked up and met his gaze, and for a single moment, her eyes mirrored the heat he knew was in his. Then she frowned and turned back to the instruments giving continuous readings on her progress, not missing a step.

"Macy." He took a step nearer.

"Yes?" she replied, not glancing up.

Taking any response as encouragement, he walked over to stand in front of her treadmill. "We have to talk."

"Can't see a need." Her eyes stayed fixed on the computerized readings.

He shoved his hands into his jeans pockets. "Okay, there are things I want to say."

She waved at the vacant treadmill beside her. "So talk."

He scanned the room, considering his options. They needed to talk, and if doing it this way made her comfortable, then why not? He mounted the treadmill and programmed it for the same pace as Macy's. They walked for several minutes before she said, "You wanted to say something?"

"I apologize."

There was a heavy pause when the only sound in the cavernous room was their shoes rhythmically hitting the tread. Finally she spoke, still without turning to him. "For what?"

"For everything." God knew, he'd change this all for her if he could. Protect her from the fallout.

"Everything?" For the first time since he'd entered the room, she looked at him. Her eyes held a sea of confusion and pain. He'd put that emotion there.

He gripped the rails of the treadmill until the blood supply was cut off in his fingers. "Not for making love to you. Even though I should be sorry it happened too soon, I can't be."

"Me, either," she whispered.

His heart skipped a beat. "Macy—"

"But you still want to marry me to buy my father's company."

"Yes," he said slowly, deliberately, as if that could soften the blow.

She turned sharply back to the instruments giving readouts. "We have an impasse then."

Impasse? Damned if he'd let them waste time in a deadlock, on either a business or personal level. He switched off his treadmill and whipped around to stand in front of hers, hands on hips, challenging her to look at him. "This is not over. We're in no way over, Macy."

She turned her machine off and stepped down, then strode past him toward the lifts. He followed. But instead of pressing the button, she headed for the stairwell. The gym was only two floors below their suite—she probably just wanted to run off the extra adrenaline. When they reached their floor, he overtook her and slid the key card into the lock before holding the door open for her.

Macy headed for her room, and turned at the door to her bathroom, seemingly unsurprised to find him behind her. "I need to take a shower."

He shrugged then folded his arms. "Me, too."

"You have your own bathroom."

"We're in this one."

"No, I'm in this one." She folded her arms, mirroring his pose.

Despite his serious intentions, he had to work to hold back a grin. People rarely stood up to him, challenged him to his face. He liked Macy doing it.

He leaned a shoulder against the doorjamb. "I want to spend time with you and we both need a shower. We've seen each other naked."

She sighed. "If we get into the shower together, we both know we won't be talking."

He let the grin free. "Is that a problem?"

She made a strangled sound in the back of her throat. "How can I get my head straight with you here?"

"We don't have to make love." He shrugged. "We could take turns in the shower and talk."

Her hazel eyes dismissed the suggestion. "How likely is that?"

"I can do it." *If he put in a superhuman effort.* "Are you worried about your own self-control?"

She nibbled on her bottom lip. "Maybe," she admitted.

"Let's see, shall we?" After flinging the door closed behind him, he moved past her and turned the shower on. "Who first?"

She seemed to debate as her eyes crept to the closed door and back. Then her face set, decision made, and she lifted her chin. "You."

She thought she was calling his bluff. Though, to be honest, his heart was beating so hard he was having trouble remembering what the bluff was about.

He grabbed the neck of his shirt at the back and yanked it off, watching her eyes devour his chest. Other women had appreciated his body before—he knew it had appeal—but no one had ever looked at him with the hunger Macy tried to deny. It sent every last drop of blood he had to spare straight to his groin.

He toed off his runners. "You happy to talk about the project?"

Macy cleared her throat. "Yes."

"Excellent." He undid his zipper and peeled off his jeans and boxers. "That's what this trip was for after all."

"True," she croaked, as if forcing the word out.

He stepped under the water and began to lather up, watching her watch him. No way would he believe she didn't want him to make love to her when he could see the heat her eyes were generating—enough to keep his entire house toasty in the winter.

He soaped his chest, then stomach. "Tell me about the forecasts for the first six months of operation."

She frowned, eyes not straying from the path his sudsy hand was taking. "We estimate…" Her voice trailed off as he lathered his abdomen and lower.

He held back a smile. "Macy?"

She looked at the ceiling, lips moving quickly and silently as if reciting something. Maybe he wasn't winning—maybe her self-control was better than his. He'd try harder. He soaped his face, before turning into the shower spray to rinse his eyes clear. Softly at first, then more firmly, he felt a hand on his back, tracing his spine. He turned slowly, and the hand followed, feathering around his side to his abdomen. She was still fully clothed, a slightly lost expression on her face, as if she wasn't sure what she was doing.

He was sure.

He'd never been more sure of anything.

He wrapped an arm around her waist and pulled her tight against him, under the spray. Then he stood there for seconds, minutes, he couldn't be sure, just holding her. Feeling her close. She let him, her cheek pressed against his shoulder. He could feel her chest rising and falling as rapidly as his own.

"Ryder—" she arched her neck back to look up into his eyes "—what are we doing?"

"It feels right, Macy."

"Yes," she agreed. "But *is* it right?"

"Macy, I'm not thinking about buying your father's company now. *You* do this to me." He snagged her hand and lowered it to where he ached for her. She encircled him with her fingers and he groaned. "No woman has ever affected me this much before. I'm ready for you all the time. Sometimes I can't believe I'm able to have conversations at all."

"Even when we're in business meetings?" Her hand continued to caress him, making his breath choppy.

"Especially when we're in business meetings. That blasted twist you've had your hair up in has been driving me crazy. I've had to clench my fists to stop them from reaching over and liberating your hair. And then taking you on the boardroom table."

With her free hand, she pulled the band out of her ponytail and he turned them so she could tilt back and let the water flow through her hair—changing it to liquid silk. He leaned above her as she was arched over his arm and captured her mouth, water running down them both. Could someone explode from need? His senses were hyperaware, taking pleasure almost to the brink of pain—all because of one woman. One amazing woman.

He straightened, bringing her with him, and looked deep into her eyes. "It's been this way for me from the first moment I saw you."

She reached to kiss his throat. "When we shook hands?"

"Before that." He grabbed the hem of her tank top and pulled it over her head, then threw the sodden fabric onto the floor outside the shower. "When I walked in the room and saw you."

"You didn't let it show. Though I did notice you staring." A shy smile curved her lips.

Taking advantage of her distraction, he slid his hands under the sides of her shorts and panties and slid them down, then waited as she stepped out before throwing the garments on the floor with her top.

He cupped her face. "I had this plan for you, but then I met you and I haven't been able to think straight since. That first day, tasting the chocolates you handed me—" He groaned.

A faint blush stained her cheeks. "I couldn't take my eyes off your lips that morning."

He reached behind her and unhooked her bra, flinging it onto the pile, leaving her naked, like him, the way they should be together. "I wanted so badly to do this," he rasped and kissed her again, hungrily.

Her arms wound up and around his neck, locking him in place. She swayed against him. As she moved he could feel the round softness of her breasts shifting across his skin. His arousal stroked across her belly. Her swaying was such a simple movement, but because it was Macy, it was so powerful he wasn't sure how long he'd last before embarrassing himself like a teenager.

Holding her shoulders, he maneuvered her against the tiled wall where the warm water flowed over them. He grabbed the soap and slid it across her shoulders, down to the slope of her breasts. Then, wanting the contact with her skin that the soap was monopolizing, he rubbed the cake back and forth in his hands until they were thickly lathered and slid his palms over her beautiful breasts, paying attention to the peaks that formed hard buds under his fingers.

He let the shower wash away the soap then leaned down to continue the task with his mouth. Macy moaned and her fingers speared through his hair.

He rested his cheek against the sweet swell of her breast and looked up. "Would it be so bad, married to me, doing this for the rest of our lives?"

Before she could answer, he let a hand snake down her belly to find the place he'd been wanting to touch since they'd walked into this bathroom. No, since he'd woken this morning.

She gasped and writhed against the wall behind her, but still managed to squeeze out a reply. "Marriage is about more than good sex."

He slipped two fingers inside her and claimed her mouth. "Good sex?" He kissed her again, lingeringly. "Macy, sex doesn't get better than this."

"Okay," she panted, hands fisting in his hair, "phenomenal sex."

He shot an arm out of the shower and snagged his jeans, extracting a condom from his wallet and quickly sheathed himself. Then he stood before her, devouring her with his eyes, *burning* for her. "Tell me you won't want to do this again when we leave this shower."

"I can't." She reached for him, bringing him back firmly against her, her wet skin sliding against his.

"Tell me you could walk away from this, because I sure as hell can't."

He grasped her knee and brought it up around his hip and finally, *finally* thrust into her. Sensation flooded his system. Macy. The feel of her enveloping him. Macy. Her teeth biting into his shoulder. Macy. Her hips bucking against his, taking more of him inside her. Macy. The slide of their bodies in rhythm.

"Ryder," she murmured, her eyes closed. "Ryder."

Hearing his name on her lips when she was beyond thinking, when her words would be instinctive, almost made him lose control on the spot. But he gritted his teeth and held on.

"Macy, look at me." She opened her eyes and locked gazes with him. "Stay with me…because…I want you to *know*…this is just…about you…and me."

"I do know," she breathed. Then, still holding his eyes, her breath rushed out on his name and her body clenched around him, her fingers digging into his biceps, and the intensity of the embrace pushed him over his own edge where the world imploded in a cascade of fireworks and sensation.

He slumped against her, holding her tight, never wanting to let her go.

Hoping with everything in him that he never had to.

Eight

The next day, after a lazy morning in bed, Macy turned off the shower, her muscles limber and warm from the hot water, her mind focused on the memories of yesterday when Ryder had taken her beyond what she thought was possible between two people. He was right—sex didn't get better than what they had.

She stepped out onto the bathmat and found Ryder there waiting, her towel in his hand, charcoal trousers zipped but not buttoned and a grin stretched across his rugged face. Her heart melted at the gesture—simple yet endearing. "Thank you."

He wrapped the towel around her shoulders then used the movement to tug her into a kiss. "I've ordered breakfast," he said against her mouth. "It'll be here in five minutes. Then we need to talk about what we'll do with the day."

She blushed. After they'd left the gym yesterday,

they'd spent the day in his bed, ordering room service and making love until they'd fallen asleep late into the night.

She looked up into eyes that were focused entirely on her. "What do you think Tina and Bernice will say?"

"I don't know about Tina—she might have believed you when you said we'd found some other properties to investigate. Bernice on the other hand—" he grinned "—may have some suspicions since I got her to hold all calls. But she's far too professional and dignified to mention it."

Macy wrapped her hands around the towel edges she could reach. She'd rather not have anyone know that she and Ryder had moved their relationship to another level, though Bernice was bound to find out. Ryder's assistant seemed very perceptive, but he was right, she was professional. She wouldn't mention it.

She smiled up at him. "What did you order for breakfast?"

He rubbed his palms up and down her towel-covered arms, and she felt his heat through the fabric. "Strawberries, croissants, juice and coffee."

"Perfect."

"I can think of more delectable treats—" he leaned in to kiss her earlobe "—but this will do for now. I'll give you a couple of minutes to get dressed."

When he left, the bathroom seemed colder, the colors lackluster, the air flat. She drew in a sharp breath and held it, considering what that meant. In a short time, he'd become the brightest thing in her life. The idea of being without him seemed dull and lifeless, a path that made her stomach clench to even consider. Warily, she met her own eyes in the mirror. Was she in too deep?

A knock sounded at the door outside and voices

brought her attention back. Room service had arrived. She pulled on clothes for the first time in almost twenty-four hours and went out to the suite's dining room.

Breakfast was laid out on a table at the window overlooking Sydney. But Ryder was frowning, his shoulders tense. He clenched a rolled newspaper in his fist.

Uneasy, she went to him and laid a hand on his forearm. "What's happened?"

He looked up, startled, then his eyes filled with a dark pain. "Macy..."

Her stomach fluttered—something was very wrong. "Ryder, tell me."

He rapped the rolled newspaper into his other palm, then again, as if deliberating on how to tell her. A hundred possibilities ran through her mind, each worse than the last, but still he didn't speak. She lifted a hand to his face, bringing his focus to her.

He swallowed, his Adam's apple bobbing down then up. "They're carrying a story on us. Being here."

"But the media knew we're staying here on our business trip." There had to be more to it than that, so she waited.

"They're saying we're, quote, holed up in our room."

"Oh." Her stomach swooped and she gripped the back of the chair beside her. She'd been so happy this morning when she'd woken in Ryder's arms. Warm, secure and blissful.

Ryder guided her into the chair and crouched in front of her, gripping her hand with his free one. "They have a source from the hotel saying we've barely left our suite. We're ordering room service and not letting housekeeping in."

She felt sick. It had happened. She was back to being a gossip-media target. All the running and hiding and playing the model citizen all these years had been for nothing.

Ryder swore, low and hard. "I'll sue the hotel."

"Show me the story."

He opened the page and held it out. The headline screamed Love Nest. She skimmed the article—mainly innuendo and speculation, but enough to put her straight back on the radar of gossips and magazine editors.

Ryder stood, his face filled with self-recrimination. "I did this. *Damn it*, I caused this by coming here."

Slowly, she stood, the truth of their situation becoming clear. "Well, I'm glad you did." Her breath was shallow, her heart still fluttered with the fear of the upcoming media frenzy, but she made herself stand calmly so she could explain.

"How can you say that?" His features twisted, disbelief patent.

"Ryder, this is just about my worst nightmare, but I can't bring myself to regret this, all that we've shared."

Then it hit her, she was in love.

She could put up with being the subject of a newspaper story to have him. She would put up with more. Even—she swallowed past a ball of emotion in her throat—a marriage of one-sided love if it gave him what he wanted most. Her father's company. She could do it. She *would* do it. She would do it for him, the man she loved.

Ryder was eyeing her skeptically. "Tell me why you're taking this so well. You realize they'll follow us like hyenas now?"

Macy bit down on her lip as her stomach churned, glad she hadn't eaten yet because the idea of being stalked by the media made her nauseous. "I know."

"Then explain this to me, because I have to tell you, your reaction makes no sense whatsoever."

"This—" she waved the newspaper "—doesn't matter." She threw it down on the table and straightened her spine. "Ryder, I've decided to marry you."

His eyes narrowed. "Because we were caught out?"

"No, because I've made a decision." Her hands were trembling, so she folded her arms tightly under her breasts to hide them. "You've put up some very persuasive arguments—" *and I love you* "—and I want you to have my father's company. I'll take you up on your offer to give me a CEO's position with Chocolate Diva or one of your other companies—" *so you don't guess why I'm doing this* "—and you'll take another step toward gaining control of your board of directors. A win-win."

He stared into her eyes, his face inscrutable. Macy held her breath, waiting for his reaction. She'd expected him to be pleased. Keen. Why wasn't he pleased? Her skin went cold. He'd changed his mind.

Then he shook his head and held up his palms. "Macy, I don't want to push you into something you don't want to do just because you're upset about bottom-feeder reporters."

Relief flooded through her veins. He still wanted to marry, he was just concerned for her. She smiled to convince him, ignoring the warning signals in her mind that danger lay ahead. She would do this for him.

"I'm one hundred percent sure. Pour the coffee and let's drink to it."

He rubbed a hand over his puckered forehead. "You're serious."

"You bet I am," she said, meeting his eyes with certainty.

* * *

Ryder poured the coffees and juices, and used the silver tongs to put a croissant and several strawberries on each plate. He needed the time to readjust since the earth had just shifted under his feet.

He'd done it, he'd moved a huge step closer to controlling Bramson Holdings.

But at what cost?

He was condemning his sweet Macy to a marriage like his parents'—loveless. He cared for her, even more so now that they'd been intimate and she'd allowed him to see her vulnerabilities. He genuinely liked her, as well as desiring her like all hell.

Yet he was condemning her to his mother's fate.

What kind of monster did that make him?

She went to sit at the breakfast table, as if the decision was made, but he grasped her hands and stayed her. "Macy, I know this is what I wanted, but I need you to be absolutely certain. Can you be truly satisfied with this arrangement?"

Her smile faltered for a fraction of a second—he would have missed it if he hadn't been watching so attentively. But then her smile was wide when she spoke and he wondered if he'd imagined it.

"You asked me yesterday if it'd be so bad being married to you, making love with you for the rest of our lives. It was a good point. This will be good for our careers, and we get phenomenal sex to boot. It sounds like a great deal and I'd like to take you up on it."

He pulled her close and wrapped his arms around her, thanking the heavens for this, for her, for everything. "I don't deserve you."

She pressed a kiss to his neck. "You deserve all

good things," she whispered. "Starting with my father's company. Ring him."

Ryder checked his watch and did the conversion to New York time. It was night there. He had to admit, there was a lot of appeal to the idea of ringing Ian Ashley now and getting things underway. "You sure you don't want more time to think about it?"

"I'm sure. Ring him."

He snatched up his cell phone and found the number then punched it out on the hotel phone so he could put it on speaker.

It rang several times before a gruff voice filled the room. "Ashley."

"It's Ryder Bramson." He snagged Macy's hand and interlaced their fingers, wanting her to know they were a team in this. "I'm calling to tell you I've met your condition of sale."

There was silence on the line. "Really? That was quick."

"Macy is here with me now in fact."

He raised his eyebrows and inclined his head to the phone. Macy shook her head. He nodded, understanding—he hadn't thought she'd want to talk to her father.

"I'll have the papers delivered to you by the morning." Ryder had them drawn up with his signature before he'd left the States, and one of his staff was waiting for the word to deliver them.

"Right," Ashley replied. "Good. I'll look out for them."

Ryder hung up the receiver and squeezed Macy's fingers. "It's done."

"It's done," she repeated softly and smiled.

He pulled her back to the couch and sank down with

her on his lap, tucking her in against his chest. "I promise, I'll always look after you. I'll be faithful and I'll do my best to make this marriage work." *I'll never be like my father,* he vowed to himself. This might be a loveless marriage, but that didn't mean they had to end up hating each other. Or hurting each other.

"I know you will." She wrapped her arms around his waist and snuggled in. "I trust you. You're a good man, Ryder Bramson."

Was he? When he'd convinced a gorgeous woman with the world at her feet to marry him so he could get his hands on more money and power? He shut his eyes as if that could stem the self-disgust that was threatening to overwhelm him. But he pulled Macy closer. He couldn't give her up. It wasn't just the money anymore. He needed Macy in his life, in his bed.

And he'd make sure he lived up to the faith she'd put in him if it killed him. Starting now.

"Let's go back to Melbourne today," he murmured. "As much as I want to stay here in bed with you, we have plans to make. Besides, now you've agreed to be my wife—" he kissed one eyelid, then the other "—we have every night for the rest of our lives to make love."

She sighed happily. "I could get used to that."

Hell, so could he. But this was about more than their bed. It was also about her future happiness and nothing was more important than that.

"I'll make this work, Macy," he whispered into her hair. He had to, for her sake.

As they stepped into the executive jet terminal at Melbourne's Tullamarine airport, Ryder took Macy's hand and squeezed it. She looked up at him and smiled, and when they paused to wait for their bags to be collected, she leaned in to him. The gesture was nothing extraordinary, but it was so loaded with meaning, with trust and faith, that an air of contentment descended over him and seemed to envelope them both.

His phone beeped and he checked the message. "The car's here," he said. The driver he'd put on retainer for his Australian trip was meeting them. "I'd like to drop into the office first."

She nodded. "Suits me. I want to check on a few things there."

He wasn't surprised she was happy with the plan; she was as much a workaholic as him. He liked that about her. "I'll get the driver to drop us then take our bags to your apartment."

She looked at him with a question in her eyes. Now he knew what it was to have her in his bed, he wasn't planning on sleeping apart tonight. "I thought you'd be more comfortable if we stay at your apartment than my hotel room."

A slow smile spread across her face. "You thought right."

They reached the limousine and the driver took their bags from Ryder and opened the back door for them.

"Ryder," she said once they were settled in the car and he'd draped an arm across her shoulders.

He looked down at her and his blood heated. "Yes?"

"I'm having a thought about the office that's inappropriate for the workplace." Her eyes twinkled.

"I think I'll like this thought. Tell me about it."

"I have to warn you. It's very unprofessional."

"We've both spent far too much time being professional over the years." As soon as they'd spent half an hour at the office—one hour tops—he was taking Macy to her apartment and making love to her again. "I vote for your idea."

"You haven't heard it yet."

"Does it involve you and me?" He raised an eyebrow.

"Yes."

"Does it involve clothes?"

She grinned. "Definitely not."

"And it's set in the office?"

"Yes."

"Then I love it. You can tell me the details as I need to know." Maybe they wouldn't make it back to her apartment. Maybe they'd use his desk—it'd seemed fairly solid.

He smiled, marveling at his luck to be marrying this woman with her business exterior covering a burning passion underneath. He couldn't wait for the wedding.

He kissed the top of her head and spoke with his lips against her hair. "Have you thought about what sort of wedding you'd like?"

"Not really," she said. "Remember, I only agreed to this a few hours ago."

"True, but I want to get moving on it quickly." He needed that marriage certificate ASAP to buy Ashley International and get the Bramson Holdings stock. "Do you have a preference for Australia or the States?"

She considered a moment. "I have no real ties to either. Will you want your mother at the wedding?"

He imagined his mother's reaction to the news. "She'd never forgive me if we did it without her," he said dryly. "She'll want to plan it and welcome you into the family properly—probably even want to host it but I'll talk her out of that if you want."

"I don't mind. I think it's sweet that she loves you that

much." There was something in her eyes that he couldn't define. Perhaps wistfulness. Perhaps longing.

He thought again of the young girl she'd been when she'd lost her own mother. A knife twisted in his gut, thinking of his Macy struggling through something like that. Especially when she'd been so young. And alone, without her father's support.

He traced a pattern on her arm where his hand rested. "I wish I could have met your mother."

A deep pain flashed in her eyes, though she masked it quickly. "She would have liked you."

If she'd been anything like Macy, he'd have liked her, too. But the rest of her family was another matter. A sister who'd probably been the one to leak the story of the sale condition to the press, and a father who'd made the condition of sale in the first place. How that excuse for a family had produced a gem like Macy was beyond him.

But they were still her family, and so he asked, "Will you invite your father and sister to the wedding?"

She didn't say anything for a long time, then said softly, "Yes. But not many people. I don't want anything grand."

"Or involving the media."

"Definitely not." She shuddered.

"I have a house on Long Island. The grounds are large and private, we could have the ceremony there."

She smiled. "Sounds perfect."

"We could live there after we're married if you want. It's a good place to raise a family."

Macy opened her mouth to reply, hesitated then shut it again.

"Is something wrong?" he murmured.

She drew in a shaky breath and shrugged. "It's just…

everything seems to be going so fast. This morning I was running a project in Melbourne and now I'm considering where I'll get married, and moving to New York to raise kids. Things are changing quickly."

He pulled her as close as the seat belts would allow. "The only things that have to change are the ones you're comfortable with. And if things are moving too fast, hold on to me."

She searched his eyes and he wondered what she was looking for. And if she would find it.

Breaking the eye contact, she turned her head to the side and rested her cheek on his shoulder. "How about I finish the project, we get married and after that we decide where to live?"

"Fine with me." In fact, it was more than fine with him. He knew he was getting the better end of the deal—the shares in Bramson Holdings that Ashley International owned, and a wife as incredible as Macy. He'd have children and a wife who understood he couldn't give the love most women expected. For all that, he'd live anywhere she wanted. With current technology, he could pretty much live in any city and run his company, and his private jet would ensure he was available for board meetings.

Their limousine pulled up at their office building and Ryder jumped out, and beat the driver to the other side to hold Macy's door open, ignoring the two paparazzi who'd guessed their destination.

He walked her to her office door, still holding her hand.

"Oh, good," Macy said and walked to her desk. "The chocolate arrived while we were gone."

"We need more chocolate?" he asked.

She pulled a letter opener from her top drawer and

began slitting the packing tape. "It's our own chocolate modified for the Australian market."

Curious, he took a step closer. "Modified?"

"We're experimenting." She lifted a block from the packing. "I'll heat some of each and show you."

"Sure." He left Macy pulling out packages and walked down the hall to his own office. He fell back into his chair and booted up his computer, scanning the messages Bernice had left on his desk. Then his attention snagged on his desk and he grinned. He thumped it a couple of times, testing its strength. Yep, it was solid enough to take his and Macy's weight. His pulse picked up speed and he leaned back in his chair, lacing his fingers behind his head. He was going to enjoy being married. He had a solid desk in New York, too.

His Web home page welcomed him and he clicked on his usual round of U.S. newspapers, focusing mainly on the financial pages, but one story in the sidebar caught his attention. His name. And Macy's. And a photo of them leaving Sydney only a few hours ago.

He clicked on it, his stomach sinking. Surely the papers had more famous people to stalk. Yet here in glorious color was the photo of them kissing in her apartment foyer two weeks ago. And them in Sydney this morning along with the heading, Bramson and Ashley Emerge From Love Nest.

He scanned down, seeing the usual rumors and gossip that were associated with their names, including one on Jesse's death and another one headed Macy Finally Gets Her Man and an old photo of a teenage Macy looking painfully shy beside her sister, who was glammed up and posing for the camera.

"Bottom feeders," he muttered. These sorts of stories were one of the reasons Macy hadn't wanted to get involved with him. He was a lucky man that she was willing to put up with it for his sake and he'd make damn sure she suffered as little as possible on his account after they were married.

He stood and stalked to the window, sinking his hands deep into his pockets. "I'll protect her," he vowed to the city below.

There were only two important things in this situation—getting the Bramson Holdings stock and protecting Macy.

Nine

Ryder headed down the hall and found Macy in the lunchroom's kitchenette, stirring two pots on the stovetop with a wooden spoon. She looked the same as when he'd left her only a quarter of an hour before, yet her beauty still hit him hard and fast in the chest. Her glossy dark hair hung free over her shoulders, her shapely legs visible beneath her above-the-knee skirt. He leaned a shoulder against the doorframe, just watching. Wanting.

But there would be time for that—right now he had to show her what he'd found. He cleared his throat and pushed off the doorframe. "Macy, there's something you need to know."

She looked up, her eyes cautious. She must have noticed the serious note in his voice. "Yes?"

"There are more headlines about us—the papers are scraping the bottom of the barrel to get stories. And I expect the frenzy to increase leading up to the wedding. But I'll do what I can to protect you."

She lifted her chin a fraction of an inch. "I appreciate the thought, but I'll be all right."

He didn't doubt it. She was a strong woman. But he'd still do all that was humanly possible to protect her from as much media exposure as he could.

His cell phone rang in his pocket. He recognized the number on the screen as that of the executor of his father's will, Pia Baxter. It was early in the morning in New York, which was unusual for a business call.

As unusual as receiving three calls in two days from her.

"Excuse me," he said to Macy, then braced himself and thumbed the button. "Good morning, Ms. Baxter."

"Good morning, Mr. Bramson. I'm afraid I have more unwelcome news."

Ryder winced. "Go ahead."

"I've received correspondence from the lawyers of a man claiming to be a fourth son of Warner Bramson."

He swore low and hard. "I suppose he's planning to challenge the will?"

"It appears that way."

"Why now?" he asked, frowning. The will had been read more than a month ago.

"I'm sorry, but I don't know."

His gut clenched tight. If the will was held up by a court case, it could be years before he got the stock his father had left him. "Have you spoken to him yourself?"

Pia hesitated. "I've received a letter from his legal team overnight. I think it might be better if we keep the correspondence contained to those channels at the moment. Unless you specifically want me to speak to him."

"No, that sounds reasonable." Ryder rubbed a finger across his forehead and sighed. "Have you told Seth?"

"He'll be the next phone call I make after this one."

It seemed it was time he finally had a conversation with his half brother. If there was to be a claim—either from the real, biological offspring of his careless father, or some money-grabbing opportunist—it'd be better dealt with by a united front. "Ask him to ring me when you're done. We need to discuss this."

"Not a problem," she said.

Strategies and tactics swirled through his brain, and the odd thought that he and Seth were on the same side for the first time in their lives. He let out a breath. "Thank you for letting me know straightaway."

"You're welcome, Mr. Bramson."

He disconnected and dropped the phone with a clatter onto the lunch table. Macy looked up. "Problem?"

"It's possible my father sowed his wild oats farther and wider than we realized. Either that or the fortune-seekers are coming out of the woodwork."

Her brows rose. "Someone's making a claim on his will?"

He rolled his neck from side to side, releasing the tension that had taken up residence there. "It looks that way."

"You lose a brother one day and might get a new brother or sister the next." She smiled with sympathy. "That's certainly a roller coaster."

"A brother, assuming there's a genetic basis to the claim. It's a man. Or a boy, I guess. Who knows when the old man went out and procreated? Or how many times." Ryder shook his head, his blood beginning to simmer. "There may be claims yet to come in from all over the country."

She cocked her head to the side. "You're angry at your father."

"You bet I am." Ryder felt resentment rise up from low in his gut until he had to clench his jaw to hold it back. "He humiliated my mother for years with his mistress Amanda Kentrell. Having two sons with her and spending more time with that family than he ever spent with us." He shook his head—he'd never understand that man's actions. "My mother has lived in a constant state of shame over a man who was never capable of love and yet pretended to marry for love's sake."

"That's why you think you're not capable of love, isn't it?" Her hazel eyes zeroed in, evaluating.

"I'm self-aware enough to know I'm more similar to him than I'd like to be," he said, voice tight. He hated that knowledge, hated admitting it.

She flicked her hair over her shoulder with a quick twist of her wrist and stepped forward. "What is it that you think you and he are missing that means you can't love?"

He didn't hesitate, didn't blink. "The capacity."

"And you think you're somehow genetically different from the rest of the planet?"

He scrubbed one hand through his hair. This was the last topic he wanted to be talking about, ever, let alone when there was a threat to his inheritance. But she'd agreed to marry him and she deserved an answer to this. And it was only fair that he be very clear so she didn't harbor illusions about him.

He leaned a hip on the lunch table and focused on his future wife. "Maybe I was born this way, maybe I learned it young from him—it hardly matters at this point. But I'm not the only one. Have a look around at the world—there are lots of people without an open heart."

A frown line creased her forehead but she nodded in understanding. "I can see you believe it."

He *knew* it. But he wouldn't argue semantics. "My father tricked my mother by pretending to love her, when he only wanted her money. She's from an old and wealthy family and he used her money for his first expansion of BFH."

Macy's eyes widened. "That's awful."

It was beyond awful—it was one of the worst wounds a person could inflict on another human being. He caught her hand. "The difference is I've been up-front with you, Macy. I've never promised you what I can't deliver—love."

She gave him a sad smile and nodded her agreement. "I appreciate your honesty."

That smile ate at his heart. He pulled her to him, holding her tight, allowing himself the indulgence of having her in his arms even as his cell phone buzzed against the lunch table.

After several rings, he kissed the top of Macy's head and stepped back. "That should be my half brother. I need to take it."

Macy turned to the chocolate, her hair spilling to the side and covering her face. "Go ahead."

He grabbed the cell and thumbed the answer button. "Bramson."

"It's Seth Kentrell." The voice was unfamiliar but there was still something recognizable in the tone. Though perhaps that was his imagination.

Ryder looked out the window at the stormy Melbourne skyline. "You've heard."

"I wondered if the gold diggers would emerge with their hands out," Seth said wearily. "I rang my lawyers after Pia Baxter's call, and I've given them a quick heads-up."

Ryder drew in a controlled breath as he put aside a lifetime of memories and feelings. "You and I should meet. We need to be on the same page on this."

There was a heavy pause and Ryder wondered if his brother would rebuff the olive branch, but finally Seth cleared his throat. "I suppose it couldn't hurt to liaise. When are you thinking?"

He glanced at Macy as she stirred the chocolate, not meeting his eyes.

"I'm in Australia, but I'll see if I can get on a flight tomorrow. I'll ring you when I land and we'll arrange something."

"I'll ensure there's room in my schedule."

"One more thing." Ryder's jaw clenched. Should he even be asking this? He closed his eyes and asked anyway. "Have you had Jesse's funeral or will I make it?"

There was a quick intake of breath down the line. "If you get a flight tomorrow, you'll make it," Seth said slowly. "Our mother's been in England with her sister, so we delayed the funeral."

"Right."

Ryder had a moment's hesitation, wondering how to end the first call he'd had with his half brother, but settled on a simple "We'll talk then." He thumbed the button off, then scrolled through his list of numbers until he came to Bernice.

Macy listened to Ryder ask Bernice to get him on a plane to America as soon as possible and felt as if she was falling. He was going back to the U.S. so soon…and alone.

As he talked she absentmindedly kept stirring the

chocolate on the stovetop with her free hand. Of course he wouldn't think to ask her along on family business—they were planning a marriage of convenience, nothing more. He'd told her not more than five minutes ago that he wasn't capable of love. Any illusions she'd been harboring about finding a true partnership in the marriage were just that—illusions. And the thing was, she'd expected it. She'd *known* she shouldn't get attached to him, *known* people always pull away, distance themselves. Her father and sister had, and here was Ryder doing it before they were even married.

Ryder hung up and slipped the phone into his pocket.

She moved back to the stovetop to stir the chocolate, using the opportunity to look at the pots instead of Ryder's face, gaining a modicum of space to think.

"Why are you melting chocolate?"

She blinked and looked down at the pans. "To show you the difference in the original chocolate and a modified version we're testing for the Australian market. It has a higher melting temperature."

"Well, I'm here." He moved behind her and wrapped his arms around her waist. "Show me."

She leaned back into his solid warmth, his musky scent surrounding her, and for one moment she wished the rest of the world would evaporate, leaving just the two of them. Like it had been in Sydney, where they could make love all day, share meals, talk, laugh.

But she needed to change the rules of their relationship. She straightened away from him, missing his warmth already. "I hardly think now is the time." She switched both stovetop elements off. "You must have things to do—pack, make plans."

"Nothing I can't handle. Show me the chocolate."

She surveyed his face. No signs of strain despite the stress he must be feeling. If he was willing to go as far as marrying her for the stock to get control of Bramson Holdings, then having an extra claimant to the will must be devastating. He was blocking out the problem. Perhaps he even wanted a distraction for a few minutes before facing the disaster awaiting him.

But—her heart clutched tight—she could barely get her mind to focus on anything except the fact that he was leaving in mere hours without her.

"Macy, show me the chocolate." His tone was deep and hypnotic.

She swallowed hard and nodded, not sure she could trust her voice. She checked the thermometers in both pans and gathered herself. "They're at the same temperature." She dipped a spoon in one pot and let the chocolate run off back into the pan, feeling Ryder watching over her shoulder. "This is the original Diva chocolate as it's sold in the U.S."

"Right."

Then she lifted the spoon in the other pot and let the more viscous chocolate run off. "This is the modified version. It's thicker because it has a higher melting point. It can keep its structural integrity better on the retail shelves in the hot Australian climate." She dropped the spoon back in. "But I don't want to talk about this. I want to talk about your trip."

He leaned in beside her ear and whispered, "I don't."

A delicious shiver ran down her spine and she bit down on her lip to hold back a moan. "You need to pack and sort through the things on your desk. You're leaving in a matter of hours."

He pressed a kiss to the side of her throat. "And I'll

miss you while I'm gone. I won't be thinking of much of anything else but you."

Part of her wanted to believe him. The part that loved him, that couldn't imagine being without him. But her rational mind wouldn't be fooled—he hadn't even considered taking her with him. "You'll survive just fine."

He took the spoon from her and dipped his finger in the chocolate, coating the end, then he turned her in his arms and smeared the thick chocolate on her bottom lip. "That depends on your definition of survive."

His face descended and he licked her lip, before sucking it into his mouth. She went dizzy for a moment but then made herself lean back.

"I'll miss you, too." She'd miss him more than she'd ever missed anything or anyone. The thought left her lost, adrift. In the short time she'd known him, he'd become like an anchor in her life.

Her stomach hollowed. Was she crazy? She'd fallen in love with a man who, like her father, could turn his emotions on and off at will. Who could say he didn't know how he'd survive without her, but hadn't for a second considered taking her with him.

Sure, he desired her now, but how long would that last? And then what would they have left? She had a vision of her loving him, yearning for him, and watching Ryder change back to The Machine in their home, and tears stung the back of her eyes.

He took a smudge of chocolate from the spoon in the second pan and wiped it on her lip. "I don't know how I'll last. I need you so much right now I'm ready to explode. If the trip wasn't for this funeral and meeting my brother, I'd whisk you away and take you with me. Now hold still while I test the difference between the two versions."

His mouth covered hers as he tasted her lip again. Her blood pumped frantically through her veins, making her light-headed. Her senses swam. She let go of her doubts and gripped the front of his shirt, holding him to her, needing nothing more than this kiss, wanting him closer, closer. Especially if she wouldn't have him forever.

When he pulled away, his breath was coming hard and he leaned his forehead on hers. "Interesting," he said, his voice thick, "but I'm not sure I got the full effect."

With one hand, he leaned to take the spoon from the first pot, and with the other hand, he undid three buttons on her blouse. He spread the warm chocolate at the base of her throat and when his hot mouth covered the spot and sucked, she couldn't help but moan and arch back.

But when he'd taken all the chocolate from her skin, he turned back to the pots of thickening chocolate and began to stir to coat the spoon. In those moments, some reasoning returned.

She was setting herself up for heartache. It was one thing to agree to sign a marriage certificate so he could buy her father's company. It was another to participate in this charade, pretending they could have a real marriage when her fiancé believed he was incapable of love. She'd never survive a half marriage with a husband she loved but who kept her at a distance.

With startling clarity, she saw what she had to do—this needed to be a paper marriage only. No children, no living together, no illusions. No broken heart.

They could marry and he could buy her father's company and acquire the stock he wanted. But she couldn't let her heart be dragged along indefinitely. That had already happened once when she was young and grieving for her mother, and her father chose to lavish his affection on her sister, all but ignoring her. She wouldn't survive it again, especially not from Ryder.

The only way to protect herself was to ensure distance between them. He could have his life in the U.S. and she'd carry on her life in Australia. All that would connect them would be a simple piece of paper, and after the marriage contract was in place, they would never need to talk—anything on a personal level would be at an end. They could marry on paper but live their own lives.

Ryder turned back to her, and she put a staying hand on his hard chest. "Ryder, we need to talk about our marriage. There are some things I think we need to do differently."

"Later." He moved her hand and pulled her blouse across to expose one shoulder and kissed it with his open, hot mouth.

Her bones began to slowly dissolve. But she found the strength to whisper, "Wait."

He pulled back, the question in his eyes.

She was torn. They had to have this conversation, no question. But from the moment she changed the rules and Ryder agreed to a paper marriage only, things would be different. There would be no conversations on non-work topics. No getting-to-know-you lunches. No being in the same country.

No lovemaking.

He placed a soft kiss on her exposed shoulder, not pushing, still waiting as she'd requested.

She was going to give this up. Give him up.

But—she bit down hard into her bottom lip—she *could* have him one more time. Let him make love to her this last time before they had the discussion that would rule out intimacy forever. He was worshipping her body with the chocolate and his mouth, she'd be crazy to stop him now and discuss them living apart, never doing this again.

To cut short their last time together.

She moistened her lips and whispered, "You're right. We can talk later." Then she ignored everything else and focused on the man in front of her.

He undid more buttons and daubed chocolate on her stomach before licking it off. She almost melted into a pool of desire.

"You know," his voice rumbled, "I was never really a chocolate fan before, but I get it now."

He gripped the pencil skirt at her hips and smoothed it up her body until it reached the height of her panties, then he lifted her onto the lunch table.

Her heart beating hard and fast, she reached for him. "I have to admit," she said, "its appeal is increasing."

It wasn't the time for talking or goodbyes. She gave in to her body's heated insistence and pulled his head down, claiming his mouth, claiming all of him. Because the time for goodbyes would come too soon, and she'd take every moment of heaven on offer before it arrived.

Ten

Macy sat at her desk the next day, pen tapping a beat on her jotter, ostensibly working on projected figures, but in reality she couldn't drag her mind away from Ryder's flight in a few hours.

Yesterday, after Bernice had confirmed his ticket, they'd walked to her apartment and made love into the evening until Ryder had left at 2:00 a.m. She hadn't seen him for more than a few minutes at a time since—he'd been locked in meetings all day, preparing to leave. *Leave.* Her heart missed a beat and her pen stilled.

From the corner of her eye she caught movement in her doorway and looked up to see Ryder crossing to her desk. Her breath hitched as it always did when she saw him, so tall and solid and *hers.*

But he *wasn't* really hers. Her stomach clenched as she remembered he never would be. Not in the way she wanted—needed—him to be. Which was why she had to end the charade of pretending they would have a real marriage. And do it before he left tonight.

Hands clasped, he raised his arms above his head, stretching. Banishing thoughts of a bleak future where they'd be connected by nothing more than words on the page of a contract, Macy instead watched the way his muscles moved under his pale blue shirt as he straightened the kinks.

His hands came to rest on his hips and he gave her a weary smile. "How about we get out of here?"

She frowned. They didn't have any outside appointments scheduled. "Where do you want to go?"

"Your place. Somewhere else." He came around to her side of the desk and leaned back on its edge before snagging her hand. "I don't mind."

Drawing her eyes from their interlaced fingers, she checked the clock on her computer screen. "It's five o'clock."

"Which is your contracted finishing time."

She leaned back in her chair. "One that neither you nor I ever leave by."

"Then it's time we did." He gave her the weary smile again.

She studied his features. Dark smudges under his eyes matched his face's slightly weathered look. He was tired. Of course, so was she—they hadn't had a full night's sleep since they'd first made love in Sydney. They were probably both averaging three hours a night.

But it was more than that. He was worried about the new claimant to his father's will more than he wanted her to know.

She wound their fingers tighter. "You don't want to pack for your flight?"

"I'm already packed and checked out of the hotel." He

stood, tugging on her hand, and tugging at her heart just as strongly.

She couldn't refuse—not when she'd be losing him so soon. She switched off her computer and pulled on her jacket as she listened to Ryder telling Tina they were going. When she met him at her office door, he put his arm around her shoulders and she leaned in to his heat and strength. How would she survive when he left? She'd been fine before he arrived, but now she knew he was out there, now she loved him, how would she get through her days? Or nights?

Their staff bustled back and forth around them, continuing with the workday, but Ryder ignored them and pulled her closer. As they waited for the elevator, she wrapped an arm around his waist and decided not to think about him going. She'd once lived her whole life in perfect control—it'd been slipping since the moment she'd agreed to go on a date with her boss. Now it was time to give it up completely and live in the moment.

To appreciate this man for the time she had him.

They walked next door, past the sounds of the city and the traffic, and up to Macy's apartment. As Ryder loosened his tie, she dropped her bag on the phone table and pressed the play button on her answering machine to hear the message that flashed. Her father's voice filled the room, congratulating her on her upcoming marriage, followed by her sister passing on similar sentiments.

Ryder scowled. "They should be apologizing to you, not congratulating you."

She slid out of her black slingbacks and picked them up by the straps. She knew he was annoyed at her sister for leaking details to the media, but her father? "This is the deal you made to help you gain control of your company. I thought you approved."

Ryder scowled again, hands on hips. "I only agreed because the stakes were so high. But he's your father—he shouldn't have had the clause written in the first place. And then to not tell you is worse. I can't imagine doing something so abominable to our daughter."

Our daughter. The idea hit her with the weight of a sledgehammer. But there would be no daughters or sons for them. She had to tell him soon. But looking at him now, with his indigo blue tie hanging loose and askew, Macy didn't want to talk anymore. She wanted to grab him by the tie and drag him down the hall to her bedroom for what might be their last time together. Her lungs began to labor at the thought. It'd been almost eleven hours since she'd last touched his naked skin, and her fingers quivered with the need to trace the muscles of his shoulders and arms, to kiss them.

Ryder's gravelly voice interrupted her chain of thought. "I made a reservation for dinner—I'd like to do something special with you tonight, and Tina assured me it's a very romantic restaurant. Are you up to going out?"

No, her body screamed. She'd wanted to stay home and relearn the planes of his chest, to feel his body slide against hers. But perhaps the very depth of her need for his was a warning that it would be much more sensible for them to talk somewhere else. If they stayed in, they wouldn't leave her bed, and she only had a short window of time to tell him about the changes she wanted to their arrangement.

She inhaled deeply and steadied her breathing. Then she smiled. "Give me twenty minutes to shower and change and I'll be good to go."

Ryder sat with a stunning view of the Yarra River to his left and a more stunning view across from him.

He smiled at Macy as their main dishes were cleared, feeling something close to happiness. The jazz pianist on the other side of the room coaxed a rhythm from the instrument that seemed to pulse around them. Macy's low-cut lavender dress complemented her flawless fair skin and glossy dark hair, making him want to reach over and touch her. Then again, he always wanted to touch her—the only variance was the intensity of the need.

Once the waiter left, Macy picked up her wineglass and sipped before replacing it carefully on the table, both hands circling the stem. "What will you do with my apartment building when you leave?"

He stretched his legs out, feeling full and mellow for the first time in twenty-four hours. "I might sell it. Or maybe keep it—an Australian base could be useful."

Her eyes focused on the golden wine in her glass as she swirled it around and around. "I guess it wasn't a plan you thought through much when you bought it."

A slow smile spread across his face. "It was more of an impulse buy." Then something about her words caught his attention. She'd said when *you* leave. "Macy, I'm not going anywhere permanently without you. I'll be back for you as soon as I've met with Seth. Within days. Or you can come to me when you're ready."

She bit down on her lip then met his eyes. "You don't need to make me promises. I don't expect them."

His stomach hollowed. She thought he was walking away from her? From what they had? What kind of man did she think he was? Then he thought of people in her past—her mother dying when she was young. Her father emotionally betraying her. She'd probably half expected it from the beginning. He grimaced. But he'd be damned if he'd be another person to let her down.

"I'll be back for you," he repeated fiercely.

She sent him a beseeching look, her eyes shadowed. "Let's just enjoy what we have here and now."

He shook his head, incredulous. She didn't believe him. Not something he was used to—as a rule, people accepted his words as truth. But not his Macy, he thought with one corner of his mouth pulling up into a reluctant smile. No, she was her own woman.

He reached over and grasped her hands on the stem of her glass, stilling them. "This is not just about acquiring stock anymore. I like the idea of being married to you. Why would I give that up?"

"Ryder—"

He cut her off, not wanting to mince words on such an important topic. "Macy, do you want a proper marriage with me? Living together. Children. Growing old side by side," he demanded. "Honestly."

She flinched. "I don't know."

He tightened his grip on her hands. "Why the hell not? You were happy for us to have it all two days ago." He took her hands off her wineglass and pulled them to the middle of the table. "Tell me what's different between us."

Slowly she looked up to meet his gaze and he saw her eyes were glistening. She looked damned affected for a woman who was saying she wasn't sure if she wanted to get married. He held back a curse. What was going on in her head?

She ran her tongue over her lips, and he noticed the bottom one trembled. Then, as if she read his mind, she held it between her teeth for a long moment. When she released it, she'd regained her composure and her voice was steady as she spoke. "I agreed because I was swept along in the momentum. I can give you my father's company with a paper marriage, Ryder. We don't need to be in the same house, or even the same country. You don't need anything more than that certificate."

"Damn it, Macy, I need you for so much more than that. I don't know where to start, but…I think about you every minute we're apart. I want to touch you, hold you, feel your skin against mine. Sometimes I think that having you wrapped around me in the dark of night is the only thing worth living for. Don't tell me the company is all you have to give."

"They're not the sorts of things that last," she said, not meeting his eyes. "Sex isn't enough to base a marriage on."

She was wrong. Having a lifetime of experience of watching his parents, he'd become an expert at bad marriages. He and Macy stood a better than average chance of making a marriage work. No one could expect more than that going in. It was a good risk. *He* was a good risk.

He just needed to find a way to convince her of that.

He stood and held a hand out. "Dance with me."

Macy's eyes softened as she laid her delicate hand in his and stood. There were only three other couples on the floor, so when they reached the middle, Ryder took his time and held her close for a moment. She allowed him the gesture, melting into him with her beautiful softness. The scent of her filled his head, sweet and intoxicating.

Then, reluctantly and only in deference to their surroundings, he allowed a small space between them and led her in slow steps to the mellow jazz. She felt so damn good. Even on a night when his inheritance was in danger, Macy trumped everything else and filled his thoughts.

"Tell me you'll move to the States with me and have my children," he murmured near her ear.

"Please don't ask that, Ryder." Her forehead wrinkled and her hazel eyes were shadowed as they'd been when he'd said he'd be coming back for her.

He cocked his head to the side, trying to work out what was really going on. There was something he was missing and he hated being out of the loop. Especially when it concerned Macy.

He swung her around, but didn't break eye contact. "Why wouldn't I ask?"

"Because you'll only accept one answer and I can't promise that's the answer I'll give."

He blew out an exasperated breath. "Why on earth not? Give me one good reason why we can't have a proper marriage and I'll back off. One good reason, Macy, just one."

She lifted her chin and looked him square in the eye, face tense as if expecting rebuke. "Because I love you."

He stopped dancing and stood stock still in the middle of the dance floor. Other couples glided by, though none near enough to overhear Macy's shocking declaration.

Heart hammering, he cleared his throat. "Are you sure?"

"Yes," she said on a sad laugh.

His chest swelled as it filled to bursting with a powerful happiness. A gorgeous, intelligent woman of integrity like Macy loved him. *Loved* him. He had to be the luckiest man ever born. He grinned.

He started dancing again, bringing her with him across the floor, their bodies moving as one. "So why would that *stop* you from marrying me? I'd have thought that was a good sign."

She paused, almost missed a step. "It's only a good sign if both people are in love. If it's only one person, then it becomes a minefield. The marriage fills with bitterness and resentment. I don't want that to happen to us, Ryder," she ended on a whisper.

Suddenly he saw his parents' marriage through new eyes. He'd thought it was loveless on both sides, but he'd been wrong. His mother had loved his father, and his father hadn't loved her back. She hadn't just been embarrassed by his father's semi-public antics, she'd been *heartbroken*.

He closed his eyes for a moment, wishing he could have done something for his mother, even as he acknowledged it'd been far beyond his control.

Then he opened his eyes and focused them on the incredible woman in his arms. *He wasn't his father.* He'd no more leave Macy and start another family with a mistress than hack off his left arm.

Heart thumping, he pulled her close again and rested his cheek on her the top of her head. He'd find a way out of this emotional maze. He'd never failed on things he'd put his mind to in the past, and wasn't about to start now. Not when it was this important.

Since Ryder had a plane to catch, it was still early when they arrived back at her apartment. Despite her spur-of-the moment—and probably unwise—declaration, Macy had spent the night appreciating the time she had left with him, just as she'd promised herself—reveling in the feel of his arms around her as they danced, delighting in the shivers he caused as he whispered in her ear.

But they'd both grown quiet during the ride home. She'd been unable to tear her thoughts away from the prospect of losing him. She'd see him again for the wedding and perhaps occasionally after that, but this was the last time he'd really *be* with her.

Ryder's driver pulled up at her apartment building and

she felt her lips tremble as it came into view. He didn't have time to come up—would they say goodbye in the car like mere acquaintances?

Ryder stepped out of the car and circled around to open Macy's door before pulling her into a tight embrace.

"I'll just tell the driver he can go," he said against her hair.

Stunned, Macy pulled away to leave a foot of space between them. "You'll miss your flight."

"I'll catch another one. Tomorrow or the next day." His tone was offhand, but his body was rigid, his eyes intense on hers.

Yesterday he'd told Bernice it was imperative he get home as soon as possible. And now he was happy to miss the flight she'd booked? "You need to speak to your brother."

His shoulders rolled back. "I'm not leaving with things left undecided between us. We need to fix this before I go. Get back to where we were forty-eight hours ago."

A shiver passed along her body. She'd do pretty much anything to go back to where they'd been forty-eight hours ago. To the bliss they'd shared in Sydney, to the excitement of the trip home when they were planning their wedding and married life. But no one could turn back time, not even Ryder Bramson.

"That's not going to happen, whether you stay another day or not," she whispered.

His eyes were closed for a long moment and his hands thrust deep in his pockets. "Macy, we can make this work."

She swallowed hard before she was able to speak. "Ryder, I can't. I'll give you a paper marriage so you can buy my father's company, but I just can't do more than that. I'm staying here in Australia. Permanently."

He looked up and down the street and she knew he was checking for paparazzi. There were none around but he gripped her elbow and guided her into the more private foyer anyway. If people saw them having a falling out, or—God forbid—overheard the nature of this conversation, it would be all over the world within the hour. This was the worst possible place to have the conversation but she couldn't invite him up; he didn't have the time.

Ryder steered them into the same alcove where he'd first kissed her.

"You love me," he said, voice low and urgent. "Come home with me. I'll wait—we'll catch a plane together."

A little piece of her heart ripped away. She touched a hand to his chest, needing to say this but not wanting it to be an accusation. Just the naked truth. "Ryder, you'll never love me."

He flinched as if he'd been hit but he recouped and met her eyes again. "Not in the way you mean. The falling in love kind. But I care for you. That will grow to a solid relationship."

"It would be a one-sided love. How can you ask that of me?" Suddenly cold to the bone, she stepped back, wrapping her arms tightly around herself. "If you care for me, why are you setting me up to have my heart broken?"

The words slammed into him and Ryder took an unsteady step back. Was that was he was doing? Setting a woman he cared for up for pain?

No. He was *not* his father. He'd vowed to protect Macy and he'd do everything humanly possible—more—to protect her.

He gripped her shoulders. "I'd never hurt you."

"I'm not saying your eye will drift and you'll find a

mistress the way your father did. You're too…honorable for that."

A dark pain sliced through his chest. She thought honor was all that would stop him doing something so despicable? "It's not a matter of honor," he rasped. "I *couldn't* do that."

"There are worse ways." Her lashes lowered to rest on her delicate cheeks. "If you came to resent me, I couldn't stand it."

Resent her? He couldn't think of *anything* that could make him resent someone he respected as much as Macy. The dangers and obstacles she was throwing up were irrelevant. He needed to turn the conversation around. Make her see sense.

He took her hands and folded his around them. "We're getting married anyway, why don't we just give this a shot? No children until we're sure. You come live with me and if you're unhappy you leave, no questions asked."

"No," she said almost too softly to hear.

His heart pounded. He couldn't fail. "What's wrong with that plan?"

"Ryder, I'm in so deep now that I can feel my heart bleeding in my chest because you're about to get on that plane. Imagine how I'll be if I get in any deeper with you? I won't subject myself to that."

"Are you sure?" His voice grated against the sides of his throat as he spoke the words.

"If there was a chance you'd love me back, then I'd take the risk. But you won't and you know it."

A thick band of steel encircled his lungs, making it hard to draw breath. He couldn't refute it. It'd be a lie to say different. But he'd give anything in this moment to be able to say the words she needed to hear. To feel those special emotions she wanted him to return.

But he'd never love her the way she loved him. It wasn't in his nature. He didn't have her beautiful heart. Even after all she'd been through, losing her mother, suffering the emotional neglect of her father and sister, she was still able to offer him the precious gift of her heart and soul.

Suddenly, he saw himself with agonizing clarity. What the hell was he doing here, asking her to give him even more? He swore under his breath. She was right to demand he walk away, she deserved more than he was capable of giving. She deserved the sun and the moon, and every star in the night sky. She deserved a man who would love her with an open and giving heart.

Grief ripped through him, as if he was being physically wrenched in two. He had to leave. To walk away. He owed her that.

He stepped back, hating the distance already. "I'll honor your wishes," he rasped.

"You will?" She blinked up at him.

Another tear crept down her cheek and he itched to carefully brush it away. "I'll leave you to live your life and find the love you deserve."

She squeezed her eyes shut tight and pushed herself back into the wall behind her. He couldn't stand it. He'd caused this pain with his blasted plan to get control of the stock in his company. But he'd make it worse if she didn't leave.

He needed to say something. Anything. "Macy—"

She cut him off. "How do you want to do this? Get married?"

Ryder heaved out a breath. No doubt about it, she was one hell of a woman. Still willing to go through with the wedding for his sake. Once he took the shares he needed, he'd sign her father's company over to her. If she still didn't want it, she could sell it. It was the least he could do.

And in the meantime, he'd make the process as easy for her as he could. "We'll get married somewhere private and no fuss. I'll come back here and we can do it in a registry office if you want. If you want to leave Chocolate Diva now, then do it. A clean break. I'll pay out your contract and bring someone in from another subsidiary to finish up."

She shook her head, frowning. "I've never broken a contract or left a project unfinished. I'll see it out."

"These are extraordinary circumstances," he said gently.

"I'll complete the contract." Her chin went up and he realized she needed this for her pride.

It was all he could offer her in this moment—allowing her to keep her dignity. "I appreciate that. Bernice isn't leaving yet—she'll organize the paperwork for the wedding and let you know when she needs you for a signature."

She looked up at the ceiling for a long moment and when she spoke, her voice sounded as if it was coming from a long distance away. "Then I guess this is goodbye."

Not able to stand the expanse of space between them anymore, he pulled her to him and rested his forehead against hers. "I'll see you at the wedding."

She slipped her arms under his coat, around his waist, gripping his sides. "But it won't be like this again, will it?"

She was right. It would never be like this again between them. He leaned down and kissed her and she kissed him back with a touch of desperation.

Holding her face in his hands, mouths so close

their breaths were mingling, he spoke against her lips. "Goodbye, Macy."

"Goodbye, Ryder."

Then he released her, stepped back and strode out of the foyer before he changed his mind and promised her things he'd never be able to deliver.

Eleven

Ryder had been gone eight days—one hundred and ninety-one hours—which Macy had filled by working dawn till after dusk and then spending more time at the gym to ensure she fell into an exhausted slumber. But her dreams betrayed her and she spent her nights in an imaginary existence where she was still with Ryder.

Or where he left her all over again.

It was late Tuesday night when she turned the key in her apartment door and forced herself inside. She needed to move to an apartment not haunted by memories of Ryder's presence—a place he didn't own—but it wasn't practical yet. There were just under two weeks left on her employment contract and after that she'd change jobs and apartments at the same time. Maybe change cities, too. Or countries.

At least the media interest had died down after a few days. They'd taken some shots of her walking alone on the streets, run them under various headings which included words like "lonely," "sad," and "abandoned." She'd barely worked up the energy to care.

She dropped her gym bag and her briefcase and ignored the flashing light on her answering machine as she prepared for a hot shower. It'd been monumentally reckless to fall in love with her boss. Even more unwise to fall in love with a man who wanted to marry her to claim stocks in a company. But the worst of all—the crime against herself—had been to fall in love with a man who would never love her back.

They hadn't spoken since he'd left—he was honoring her wishes as he said he would, giving her as clean a break as he could. But they'd have to talk soon to arrange the wedding. Foolish though it was, their wedding was like a star of hope in the future. For one more day, she'd be with him, touch him and he'd be hers.

After toweling off and pulling on some yoga pants and a fitted T-shirt, she walked without enthusiasm through to the kitchen to see what she could scrounge up from her depleted cupboard.

The phone rang and her first impulse was to leave it for the answering machine as she'd been doing lately, but she couldn't avoid the world forever, so she picked up the cordless receiver.

"Macy," her father's voice boomed. "What did you do?"

Her stomach sank that these were the words he chose after years of no contact. She should have left the call to her machine after all.

"Do to what?" she asked coolly.

"To Ryder Bramson." His frustration practically vibrated down the line. "Last week he said you'd agreed to marry him."

Memories of that day in Sydney when she'd accepted his proposal tortured her—the naive joy that had filled her heart; the wedding plans they'd made while traveling back to Melbourne; the beautiful love-making—they crashed in on her from all sides, and she squeezed her eyes shut against the ache.

"I did," she rasped.

"Then what have you done since then to screw it up?"

Thoughts tumbled through her brain, and she tried to get a hold on the conversation's direction, but came up blank. "I have no idea what you're talking about."

"He's cancelled the deal." Her father threw the words at her like bullets and she felt her jaw slacken as she processed the information. "He's—" She stopped, cleared her throat and forced the words out. "He's not buying Ashley International?"

There was silence on the line. "You didn't know?" her father asked after a moment.

"No," she whispered. If the deal between her father and Ryder was off, the deal between her and Ryder was also off. The pain she'd been trying to keep at bay for eight days ripped open and poured through her body.

"I was sure you were behind it," he said, sounding more confused now than angry.

A cold and clammy sheen coated her skin as her body accepted the news that Ryder had severed their last link. And her father had been the one to deliver the news. She refocused on him. "Sorry to disappoint your expectations, but no."

"Macy, honey, I need you to do something for me," he said, voice now sweet and conciliatory. "Smooth things over with him. Make him go through with the sale."

If her shock had allowed, she would have laughed at

the absurdity of the request. "No one makes Ryder do anything. He's not that kind of man."

"He's refusing to take my calls, but he'll talk to you, I just know. It's important."

Despite her own pain, something in his tone alerted her to what he wasn't saying. "How important?"

He paused then sighed. "I've already committed the proceeds of the sale elsewhere."

The information was coming together to form an appalling scenario. "So if the deal doesn't go through…"

"I'll be financially ruined," he finished for her.

"I'm sorry, Dad." And even with the ill feeling between them, she truly was sorry to see anyone, especially a family member, ruined. This situation seemed to be a nightmare for everyone. "But as I said, Ryder Bramson isn't a man to be swayed if he's decided on something."

"Macy, I know I haven't been the best father to you, but I'm begging. You don't need to marry him. Tell him he can just buy it."

She gulped in a breath, stunned into holding it for two heartbeats. This was the news Ryder would have wanted to hear most—he could simply buy Ashley International and own the stock in BFH that he needed. No messy deals to marry her. But it was probably too late, now that he'd called off the deal. "I can't promise anything, but I'll try."

Trembling, she hung up the phone and leaned back on the wall behind her.

Ryder no longer wanted—or needed—to marry her. The one thing she'd had to give him was her father's company.

Now he needed her for nothing.

She slid down her living room wall, coming to rest on

the carpet, knees pulled tight to her chest. The rational part of her mind said Ryder canceling the deal to buy her father's company was a good thing, that a clean break would allow her to get over him. So why, then, did it feel as if her heart had physically been wrenched from her chest? She wanted to get out of here, to go for a run, to escape. But her legs wouldn't move. She couldn't feel them. Her hands and lips had gone numb, too.

He'd called the deal off, didn't need her, and he hadn't even bothered to tell her she'd become superfluous to his plans.

His face swam before her eyes, speaking the words he'd said the night they'd parted. *I'll leave you to live your life and find the love you deserve.* She pressed the heels of her hands against her eyes, trying to erase the finality of the message.

She'd *asked* him to leave her alone. Had he found another way to get stock in Bramson Holdings and was simply taking her at her word and limiting their contact? Or was it that she was out of sight, out of mind? A fun diversion for his time in Melbourne, but now it was over he hadn't spared her a thought?

Her heart stuttered, but no, she couldn't believe him capable of that level of callousness. He was a good man. He was trying to make this easy on her—knew he couldn't love her and was letting her get on with her own life. Which she would do. One day.

But not today.

Macy sat back in her office chair, closing her eyes against the report on her screen, the bright lights and the office itself. She hadn't yet come up with what she'd say to Ryder once it was late enough Australian time to ring him and plead her father's case. She had to try, despite knowing it would make no difference. She knew his decision wasn't about her father or his company. It was about her.

A crushing weight bore down on her from above, pressing her deeper into her chair, and she wrapped her arms tightly around her middle to stop herself breaking into a thousand pieces. Her life stretched out before her, colorless, stark, lifeless, knowing Ryder was out there in the world somewhere, living his life. He'd be occasionally in the papers, ensuring that the wound never healed. But even without the reminders, she'd never fully heal from this.

A loud, commanding knock sounded at her office door—she'd had it closed all day, an extra layer of protection from the world. She ignored it. Tina must be away from her desk, but she'd be back soon and deal with whoever was there.

The knocking came again, but she wasn't speaking to anyone today. Tina had cancelled her appointments and was holding her calls, allowing Macy to focus on the final report of their project. She'd been wanting a full day to do this anyway.

The knocks came a third time, this time accompanied by a familiar, deep voice. "Macy."

The sound of Ryder's voice sparked through her like an electric charge, at once bringing her head up to attention...*he was back*...yet causing the ache in her chest to double as understanding dawned. He'd come to explain. *Of course* his code of honor would demand he tell her in person he wasn't buying the company. That they no longer needed to marry. Knowing the truth was torture enough, but *hearing* him say the words? To have to reply coherently and wish him well in his life? Maybe even wish for him that he found the woman he could love, who could open his heart. She wouldn't be able to stand that conversation. There was no choice but to wait him out.

"Macy, Tina said you were in there."

She groaned, dropping her arms to her sides. She'd told her father that Ryder wasn't a man to be swayed. That same determination meant that now he knew she was here, he wouldn't leave until she answered. She slipped her feet into her shoes under the desk and dragged herself upright, trying to snap herself out of the shock; hoping Ryder wouldn't notice how badly she was affected.

She opened the door a fraction, but didn't dare look at him yet in case was overcome by the sudden urge to throw herself into his arms and beg him to take her back. If she kept nothing else, she'd maintain her self-respect.

She filled her lungs, held the air there a moment, then let it out in a controlled breath and met his eyes. "Ryder, I need to get this work done now. Could we talk tomorrow?"

He leant against the doorframe, bringing his face nearer, allowing his scent to envelop her. "I need to speak with you," he said, voice low. "Open the door."

Her skin quivered, reacting to his nearness, and his deep voice practically reverberated through every cell and molecule in her body. Unable to deny him much of anything when he spoke like that, yet knowing she invited more heartache, she opened the door and gestured for him to come in before closing it behind him.

She tried not to drink him in like a woman dying of thirst, but failed. His large frame was draped in a black overcoat which he tugged off and threw over the back of a chair. Then he turned and she was hit by the force of his presence—at once so familiar and yet different. His closely cropped hair begged her to touch, his full bottom lip called to her. But his beautiful eyes were shadowed and bloodshot. Everything inside her yearned to smooth the smudges beneath them with her fingers. Everything, except her sense of self-preservation.

He stepped closer but stopped, seeming uncertain. "Your face is pale." He frowned, jaw tight. "You're upset."

Tears stung at her eyes but she refused to let him see. She swallowed and blinked away any traces of moisture. "I stubbed my toe," she lied.

He raised an eyebrow, unconvinced.

She took a step back, away from the temptation of him. "I stubbed it hard."

He looked down at her bare, non-mangled toes visible in her slingbacks. "I'm sorry to hear that," he said without a trace of irony.

Her breath hiccupped in her throat. She couldn't do this—not now while everything inside her was still so raw. She swept an arm toward the door. "I really need to get this work done this afternoon. I'll call you tomorrow—"

"Macy," he interjected, his coffee-brown eyes locked on her, "there's so much I need to tell you."

Her shoulders drooped a fraction. He wasn't leaving. If she could gain herself a couple of minutes to regroup, perhaps then she could handle hearing what he'd come to say.

"Would you like a drink?" she asked with a false smile as she waved a hand toward the wet bar.

He didn't move. "I'd rather talk first."

Macy nodded wearily and faced the inevitable. They were having this conversation now whether she was prepared or not. There was only one acceptable option remaining—heading this train off at the pass.

She straightened her spine, ready to face the most

torturous discussion of her life. "I've had a call from my father. I know you don't need his company anymore."

Ryder didn't flinch. "That depends on your definition of need."

"Did you find another way to get enough stock to control your company?"

"No," he said slowly, deliberately.

She dragged in a lungful of air. He needed the stock but had cancelled the sale. He didn't want to marry her anymore. And he wanted to avoid that marriage enough to sacrifice the stock and possibly his aspirations of becoming chairman of the board. Even as the rejection struck her squarely in the solar plexus, she couldn't blame him—what man would want a wife he couldn't love, but who loved him? He'd obviously thought it through and recognized the risk of her clinging; of her holding on too tight and smothering him. And the worst of it was, she couldn't guarantee the risk didn't exist, much as she'd like to deny it.

She lifted her chin and offered him the escape he needed. "My father has another deal on the table." Her voice broke, but she swallowed and continued. "He'll sell to you without you marrying me. You can have the company, Ryder. The stock."

With not even a flicker of interest in the offer, he took a step forward. "My priorities have changed."

Stunned into stillness, she took several beats to reply. "What do you mean?"

He moved to the blue couch against the wall and held out a hand to her. "Come and sit with me."

She eyed him warily—sitting down did not equal getting this over with as quickly as possible.

"Just hear me out, Macy. If you want me to go when I'm done, I'll go." His face was earnest, imploring, and she believed him. She'd give him this one last gift of her time and attention.

She moved to the couch and sat as far away as the three-seater would allow. If he was too close, she'd be tempted to crawl into his lap and stay there. She folded her arms under her breasts, as if that could offer some protection from temptation, from what he was about to say, from the entire situation.

"I'm listening," she said in a rough whisper.

"Seth and I talked about this new claimant, J.T. Hartley, and how much of a threat he could be. I said there was a chance he really is a son of our father. The man kept a wife and a mistress for over thirty years—why wouldn't he have a second mistress, as well?"

She pressed her fingers to her temple, suddenly light-headed. He wanted to talk about his *family* when she was *dying* inside? "Please, Ryder, can we talk about this tomorrow? I can see you're tired from the trip—we can discuss it in the morning. I'll call you—"

He cut her off, his expression urgent. "You need to hear this now, Macy."

She shored up all the courage she could, and, ignoring her own pain to concentrate on the story he obviously needed to tell, she nodded. "Okay. So you think your father could have had a second mistress. Makes sense."

He flashed her a tight smile, acknowledging her willingness to listen. "Seth disagreed. He honestly believes Warner loved his mother, Amanda Kentrell."

"Then why didn't he marry her?"

He shrugged. "Respect for my mother. Fear of a scandal. Wanting to keep access to my mother's money as well as his own. Maybe my mother wouldn't agree to a divorce. Whatever it was, Seth is certain that Warner wouldn't have cheated on Amanda."

Despite everything else going on, she found herself intrigued enough to delve further. "Wasn't keeping a wife cheating on her?"

"My parents had separate lives, separate bedrooms for the few occasions when he came home. Seth's version has some possibility of being true."

She couldn't help but think of Ryder as a boy, living in that sterile family. No wonder he had imperfect notions of the capacity of his own heart. She ached to hold him and explain, but she was far from the right person to do that.

So she did what she could—focused on what he was saying in the here and now. "If you give Seth the benefit of the doubt, are you now thinking J.T. Hartley isn't a brother? That his claim will fail?"

"He'd be stupid to make a claim with nothing to back it up." Ryder scrubbed a hand through his hair, leaving the short strands mussed. "If Seth's right about Warner and Amanda, the old man could still have conceived another child after the marriage but before he met Amanda."

The media and public would go crazy for a story about a new Bramson brother, between Ryder and Seth in age and staking his claim on the Bramson billions. "Will you share the inheritance with him?"

He leaned back in the couch and lifted one ankle to rest on the other knee, seeming even more tired than when he'd arrived. "We're setting plans into place now for either eventuality. Seth is adamant that it takes more than DNA to deserve part of the company."

"What about you?" she asked, more concerned than ever about the shadows under his eyes and the stress he was under.

"To be honest, I haven't decided." His fingers began tapping on the armrest and suddenly he seemed less tired and more…as if he was…nervous. "My mind was occupied with another consequence of Seth's information."

"Which is?" If it was enough to make Ryder nervous, then whatever it was, was bigger than anything he'd mentioned so far.

"If Seth's account is reliable—" he paused, swallowed "—my father was capable of love. My view of my childhood has been recalibrated."

There was something big here, she could feel it, but she wasn't quite following. "In what way?"

"I thought my father was playing the field. Having two families, probably more. But it seems he had a woman he loved and two sons he cherished. They were his family. My mother and I were…an aberration."

Pain for him lanced through her chest. It was an awful thing to discover, no matter his age.

She leaned in, reaching for his hand and entwining their fingers. "Ryder, I'm so sorry."

He looked up at her, surprised. "I don't need sympathy—this is a good thing. Amanda, Seth and Jesse were the family he should have had if he hadn't married for money." He turned in the couch to face her. "Do you understand what this means? He was capable of romantic love. My beliefs about myself and my genes were wrong. I'm not wired against loving one woman for life. I just need to marry the one I love, the way my father should have waited to find Amanda and married her."

Her lungs stalled. The picture was beginning to come together—the call from her father, Ryder's visit today… He'd wanted to marry her for the company, the stock, the way his father had married his mother. But he realized now he should wait to find the woman he loved. And she couldn't blame him. He should have love.

She sucked her bottom lip into her mouth and bit down on it, willing herself not to cry in front of him. "That's why you cancelled the deal with my father?"

"Yes," he said, his eyes searching hers as if asking for understanding.

Another jagged piece of her heart tore away, but she didn't shrink back, she smiled. She'd let him go to find love and happiness. More than anything, she wanted Ryder to be happy. She unlaced their fingers and stood, needing to break the intimacy before she said something that revealed the depth of her pain and made him feel guilty for doing the right thing.

She headed for the wet bar and poured two glasses of water from a bottle in the small refrigerator. "I'm glad you spent time with Seth."

He followed and accepted the glass she handed him. "Just a damn shame it didn't happen before Jesse died."

He leaned back on the bar, dominating her office with his size and presence. Macy gulped her water and turned to refill her glass, speaking over her shoulder. "Did you go to the funeral?"

"Yes." He took a mouthful of water, then deposited his glass on the bar, his forehead puckered in a pained expression. "And burying a brother I hadn't known made me look at myself. Take stock."

"Understandable." She nodded, gripping her glass tightly, trying to gain strength from it, from anything, to see her through this.

"I've put things in their proper perspective now." He moved to stand in front of her. "There's something I need more than money. More than the company." He took her glass from her fingers, put it in the sink before he grasped her hands. "You."

The world tilted and she gripped his hands tighter

to avoid falling over. "Me?" Her voice was so high it squeaked. She took a deep breath, calming herself so she could speak. "I thought you cancelled the deal so you could find the woman you could love."

"I've found her." His eyes were earnest, a window directly to his heart, his soul. "And I didn't want any question in your mind about my priorities, so I cancelled the sale. Macy, I love you."

She swallowed hard. "You love me?"

"Hell, yes," he said roughly. He pulled her to him and held her firmly, and she could feel his racing heart beneath his shirt. Then he clasped her shoulders and leaned back, looking deep into her eyes. "And this is beyond business. Beyond inheritances, beyond all else—just a man in love wanting to marry his woman."

The tilting of the world, the overwhelming feeling stopped, and all she could see was his face, and hear one word repeating in her head. Her knees buckled but he grabbed her waist and held her firm. "Marry?" she whispered.

"I love you. I need you in my life. If I have to let go of the company to prove this is all about you and only you, I choose you."

She blinked up at him, unable to do much more than listen to what he was saying and try to comprehend it.

"Tell me it's not too late, Macy," he said huskily. "If my leaving killed the precious love you had, I'll never forgive myself, but I'll understand."

The uncertainty in his features, the need in his eyes brought everything back into focus and galvanized her. She laid a palm against his cheek. "Killed my love for you? Are you crazy?"

"All evidence so far would point to that, given that I was willing to leave the woman I love more than my own life." He shook his head and let out a self-reproachful growl. Then he laid his own hand over hers as it still rested on his cheek. "Tell me you love me," he said, his heart in his eyes.

A stillness came over her, a sense that the world was just as it should be, that this was *right.* "I love you."

His lips parted as his gaze darted from her eyes to her mouth and back again. "Are you sure?"

"Absolutely sure." She wound her arms up, around his neck, reveling in the shudder of his body at the touch.

"Then you'll marry me?" The rise and fall of his chest seemed to stall, as if he was holding his breath.

Macy looked deep into his eyes and felt a tear escape to run down her cheek. This man she loved with every beat of her heart loved her back with the same intensity—it was all there for her to see in his face. He brushed her tear away with a thumb and she felt another escape her lashes. She kissed him lightly, but what started as a featherlike caress of lips quickly flared into something hungrier, more passionate.

When Ryder pulled back, they were both breathing heavily. "You didn't answer my question," he said with a raised eyebrow.

"I'll marry you—" she let her hands drift across the broad expanse of his shoulders "—on one condition."

"Name it," he said, without hesitation.

Her hands flowed from his shoulders, down his arms until she found his hands. She linked their fingers, and smiled. "We don't ever spend eight days apart again. That was intolerable."

Ryder smiled back widely. "I can agree to that."

He leaned in and kissed her, and she melted, knowing she'd found her home. No matter where they lived, Ryder was, and always would be her home.

Epilogue

One month later

Macy walked into her fiancé's office, Ryder's hand at the small of her back guiding her. She looked around, impressed by its size and view of Manhattan's skyline at night. After she'd finished the Chocolate Diva project, she'd packed everything she owned and had it shipped to Ryder's house. They'd kept to their vow and only spent a couple of nights apart at a time during the transition.

This was her first visit to his office, and she ran a finger along the shelf of a wooden bookcase. "Nice setup."

"Ah," he said with a smile in his voice, "but you haven't seen the best part yet."

She turned as she heard the lock on the door click. A shiver of anticipation ran down her spine. "The best part?"

He strode across the room to the large oak desk and thumped a hand on it. "The desk. Solid enough for two."

She arched an eyebrow. "Mr. Bramson, are you flirting with an employee?"

"No," he said matter-of-factly.

"You don't class that as flirting?" She moved toward him. "You practically asked me to hop up on your desk."

"Oh, that was flirting, sure." He grinned. "It was the employee part that was wrong."

"You're firing me?" He was going somewhere with this and she couldn't wait to see where that was. Life with Ryder would never be boring.

"Well, you told me once that it's best not to mix personal and business, and I have very personal, intimate plans for you. On this very desk, in fact. I have no interest in abandoning those plans, so I have no choice but to let you go."

She didn't mention that technically, her project was over so he had no contract to "let her go" from—her report had recommended Chocolate Diva enter the Australian market and she'd handpicked a new team to take the next steps. She'd been reviewing some very attractive offers from other companies that had been impressed with her work for Ryder, and her fiancé had suggested they start their own business together, which had a strong appeal, too.

But the game was much too fun to ruin with details like fact.

She flicked her hair behind her shoulder and moistened her lips. "When you put it that way…"

"Besides—" he snagged her fingers and drew her

closer "—I have a few wedding presents that I think might make up for your shocking dismissal."

The feel of him against her, his scent surrounding her, was as intoxicating as ever. She leaned her cheek against the crisp cotton of his shirt. "I like presents. But we haven't even set a date yet."

"They're early wedding presents. You can have them now," he said slowly, seductively as he traced lazy circles on her shoulder with his thumb.

She almost purred as his hands worked their magic. "I like the sound of them already." Though nothing could be more of a present than Ryder himself. The gifts of his heart and his commitment were beyond her wildest fantasies.

"I've had your father's old company transferred into your name. All of it. Which means you also now hold stock in Bramson Food Holdings."

She felt her jaw slacken as she pulled away to look into his eyes. She'd pressed him to go through with the sale, assuring him that she knew about his priorities. He didn't need to avoid the sale to prove anything to her—she was secure in his love, and it was in both his and her father's best interests. But she'd never expected this.

"Ryder," she said, framing his face with her hands. "You wanted those shares. Keep them."

He enclosed her hands in his and brought them to his lips. Gently, he kissed each one before answering. "I want you to have them. Though—" he grinned "—I was pretty much hoping you'd use them to vote for me as chairman when it comes to that."

For a moment, she couldn't speak. He'd handed her control over his dream. For a man like Ryder, it was the ultimate vow of trust. Her heart melted. And she knew just the way to repay him.

She traced a line down his chest with one fingernail. "You'll have to play your cards right before then."

Heat flashed in his eyes. "Will this help?"

He kissed her and lifted her onto the oak desk without breaking contact, moving in to stand between her thighs.

Breathless, she broke away. "Okay, you have my vote."

He placed a kiss below her earlobe then whispered into her ear, "I'll just have to work on keeping it now."

"I'm sure that can be arranged." Her breath hitched as he drew her earlobe into the heat of his mouth. But then she remembered something. "You said wedding presents. Plural."

"Ah, yes." He straightened and cleared his throat. "This one isn't a wedding present so much as something I should have given you when I asked for your hand in marriage two months ago." He pulled a small box from his trouser pocket. "But that night I couldn't think of anything except getting back to you as fast as I could, and I was seriously amiss. Then after you'd said yes, I wanted it to be exactly the right one, so I kept looking."

He handed her the box and she opened it to find a princess cut pale blue solitaire diamond. "It's perfect," she whispered, her eyes misting up.

He slipped it on her finger and then kissed her again. "I knew I didn't want a fancy setting or other stones around it, just a strong, beautiful diamond that needed no other adornment. Like you."

She looked at the ring on her finger, then at the man who'd placed it there, and her love for him threatened to overwhelm her. She wrapped her calves around his thighs and pulled him as close as she could, needing him more than ever.

"Ryder," she whispered past a ball of emotion in her throat, "I love you."

He skimmed his hands up her thighs, his eyes drifting shut. "I love you more than I can say," he said as he lifted her skirt higher, and she lay back on the desk, dragging him down on top of her.

Much later, she pressed a lazy kiss to the chest exposed by his unbuttoned shirt. She smiled up at him. "I think I can live with those compensations for no longer being an employee." A thought occurred to her. "Now I own shares in your company, doesn't that make me one of your bosses?"

One end of his mouth twitched, and he stepped back as he began to button his shirt. "I was wondering when that would come up."

"I'll try not to use it to blackmail you."

Laughter danced in his eyes. "I appreciate it."

"I have an early wedding present for you, too." She pushed off the desk and straightened her skirt.

Ryder raised an eyebrow as he tucked his shirt into his trousers. "Cufflinks?"

"No," she said and walked over to enjoy the view from the window, knowing he'd follow.

He came up behind her and wrapped his arms around her waist. "Monogrammed golf towel?"

She grinned. "Not even close."

"Then you might want to give me a hint."

She melted back into his solid chest. "Remember the day you came back to me in Melbourne?"

"Vividly," he said, his mouth just behind her ear.

"Remember that night, back in my apartment, we became a bit…distracted, and you carried me to the bedroom?"

His arms around her tightened. "I still think about that night. And the things you did."

She'd been replaying the night over in her mind, too. As well as the nights that followed—the lovemaking since they'd committed to each other had become more intense, more beautiful. Their trust had become absolute and the effect was amazing. And it had all started with the night he came back for her.

She turned in his arms and met his warm brown gaze. "Remember we were so carried away we forgot protection?"

He stilled. "You're saying..."

"That in approximately eight months—"

He claimed her mouth before she even finished the sentence. He kissed her hungrily, possessively, and after timeless minutes, he rested his forehead against hers, breathing heavily. "That was the best night of my life for two reasons now."

"Mine, too," she whispered. "But I think we have many more best nights ahead of us."

A slow, sexy smile spread across his face. "I guarantee it," he said and kissed her again.

* * * * *

COMING NEXT MONTH

Available October 12, 2010

#2041 ULTIMATUM: MARRIAGE
Ann Major
Man of the Month

#2042 TAMING HER BILLIONAIRE BOSS
Maxine Sullivan
Dynasties: The Jarrods

#2043 CINDERELLA & THE CEO
Maureen Child
Kings of California

#2044 FOR THE SAKE OF THE SECRET CHILD
Yvonne Lindsay
Wed at Any Price

#2045 SAVED BY THE SHEIKH!
Tessa Radley

#2046 FROM BOARDROOM TO WEDDING BED?
Jules Bennett

SDCNM0910

REQUEST YOUR FREE BOOKS!

2 FREE NOVELS PLUS 2 FREE GIFTS!

Passionate, Powerful, Provocative!

YES! Please send me 2 FREE Silhouette Desire® novels and my 2 FREE gifts (gifts are worth about $10). After receiving them, if I don't wish to receive any more books, I can return the shipping statement marked "cancel." If I don't cancel, I will receive 6 brand-new novels every month and be billed just $4.05 per book in the U.S. or $4.74 per book in Canada. That's a saving of at least 15% off the cover price! It's quite a bargain! Shipping and handling is just 50¢ per book.* I understand that accepting the 2 free books and gifts places me under no obligation to buy anything. I can always return a shipment and cancel at any time. Even if I never buy another book, the two free books and gifts are mine to keep forever.

225/326 SDN E5QG

Name (PLEASE PRINT)

Address Apt. #

City State/Prov. Zip/Postal Code

Signature (if under 18, a parent or guardian must sign)

Mail to the **Silhouette Reader Service:**

IN U.S.A.: P.O. Box 1867, Buffalo, NY 14240-1867
IN CANADA: P.O. Box 609, Fort Erie, Ontario L2A 5X3

Not valid for current subscribers to Silhouette Desire books.

Want to try two free books from another line?
Call 1-800-873-8635 or visit www.morefreebooks.com.

* Terms and prices subject to change without notice. Prices do not include applicable taxes. N.Y. residents add applicable sales tax. Canadian residents will be charged applicable provincial taxes and GST. Offer not valid in Quebec. This offer is limited to one order per household. All orders subject to approval. Credit or debit balances in a customer's account(s) may be offset by any other outstanding balance owed by or to the customer. Please allow 4 to 6 weeks for delivery. Offer available while quantities last.

Your Privacy: Silhouette Books is committed to protecting your privacy. Our Privacy Policy is available online at www.eHarlequin.com or upon request from the Reader Service. From time to time we make our lists of customers available to reputable third parties who may have a product or service of interest to you. If you would prefer we not share your name and address, please check here. ☐

Help us get it right—We strive for accurate, respectful and relevant communications. To clarify or modify your communication preferences, visit us at www.ReaderService.com/consumerschoice.

SDES10R

Spotlight on

Inspirational

Wholesome romances
that touch the heart and soul.

See the next page
to enjoy a sneak peek from
the Love Inspired® inspirational series.

CATINSPLI10

See below for a sneak peek at
our inspirational line, Love Inspired®.
Introducing HIS HOLIDAY BRIDE
by bestselling author Jillian Hart

Autumn Granger gave her horse rein to slide toward the town's new sheriff.

"Hey, there." The man in a brand-new Stetson, black T-shirt, jeans and riding boots held up a hand in greeting. He stepped away from his four-wheel drive with "Sheriff" in black on the doors and waded through the grasses. "I'm new around here."

"I'm Autumn Granger."

"Nice to meet you, Miss Granger. I'm Ford Sherman, from Chicago." He knuckled back his hat, revealing the most handsome face she'd ever seen. Big blue eyes contrasted with his sun-tanned complexion.

"I'm guessing you haven't seen much open land. Out here, you've got to keep an eye on cows or they're going to tear your vehicle apart."

"What?" He whipped around. Sure enough, mammoth black-and-white creatures had started to gnaw on his four-wheel drive. They clustered like a mob, mouths and tongues and teeth bent on destruction. One cow tried to pry the wiper off the windshield, another chewed on the side mirror. Several leaned through the open window, licking the seats.

"Move along, little dogie." He didn't know the first thing about cattle.

The entire herd swiveled their heads to study him curiously. Not a single hoof shifted. The animals soon returned to chewing, licking, digging through his possessions.

Autumn laughed, a warm and wonderful sound. "Thanks,

SHLIEXP1010

I needed that." She then pulled a bag from behind her saddle and waved it at the cows. "Look what I have, guys. Cookies."

Cows swung in her direction, and dozens of liquid brown eyes brightened with cookie hopes. As she circled the car, the cattle bounded after her. The earth shook with the force of their powerful hooves.

"Next time, you're on your own, city boy." She tipped her hat. The cowgirl stayed on his mind, the sweetest thing he had ever seen.

Will Ford be able to stick it out in the country
to find out more about Autumn?
Find out in HIS HOLIDAY BRIDE
by bestselling author Jillian Hart,
available in October 2010
only from Love Inspired®.

Copyright © 2010 by Jill Strickler

SHLIEXP1010

FROM #1 *NEW YORK TIMES*
AND *USA TODAY* BESTSELLING AUTHOR

DEBBIE MACOMBER

Mrs. Miracle on 34th Street…

This Christmas, Emily Merkle (just call her Mrs. Miracle) is working in the toy department at Finley's, the last family-owned department store in Manhattan.

Her boss (who happens to be the owner's son) has placed an order for a large number of high-priced robots, which he hopes will give the business a much-needed boost. In fact, Jake Finley's counting on it.

Holly Larson is counting on that robot, too. She's been looking after her eight-year-old nephew, Gabe, ever since her widowed brother was deployed overseas. Holly plans to buy Gabe a robot—which she can't afford—because she's determined to make Christmas special.

But this Christmas will be different—thanks to Mrs. Miracle. Next to bringing children joy, her favorite activity is giving romance a nudge. Fortunately, Jake and Holly are receptive to her "hints." And thanks to Mrs. Miracle, Christmas takes on new meaning for Jake. For all of them!

Call Me Mrs. Miracle

Available wherever books are sold
September 28!

www.MIRABooks.com

MDM2819